ONE NIGHT LOVE AFFAIR

marilyn brant

Twelfth Night
Publishing

(Mirabelle Harbor, Book 5)

One Night Love Affair
(Mirabelle Harbor, Book 5)
Copyright © 2017 Marilyn B. Weigel
Twelfth Night Publishing

Cover Design © 2017 Sterling Design Studios
Editor - Hamilton Editing
Proofreader - Kimberly Dawn
ISBN-13: 978-0-9983964-0-8

DEDICATION & THANKS

Much love and thanks to my family, my good friends, and my amazing readers & early reviewers. I can't express how much I appreciate you all. This book is for YOU!

My deepest gratitude goes out to Gina Paulus, Brandy Morrison, and the awesome members of the "Mirabelle Harbor Lounge" on Facebook for loving this series and for helping me to bring out the best in every new story.

And, as always, my love to my husband and son for being so supportive, for making me laugh, and for reminding me how heroes think & talk. And also for teaching me everything I know (however little that may be!) about ice hockey.

OTHER BOOKS BY MARILYN BRANT

According to Jane

Friday Mornings at Nine

A Summer in Europe

The Sweet Temptations Collection
~On Any Given Sundae
~Double Dipping
~Holiday Man

The Perfect Pair
~Pride, Prejudice and the Perfect Match
~Pride, Prejudice and the Perfect Bet

The Road to You
The Road and Beyond (expanded edition)

All About Us (novella)

The Mirabelle Harbor Series
~Take a Chance on Me
~The One That I Want
~You Give Love a Bad Name
~Stranger on the Shore
~One Night Love Affair
~Going For It (bonus crossover novella)

Wanderlust in Suburbia and Other Reflections on
Motherhood (nonfiction essays)

NOTE FROM THE AUTHOR

ONE NIGHT LOVE AFFAIR is Book 5 in Marilyn Brant's Mirabelle Harbor series, but this book and all of the contemporary romances in this series can be enjoyed as stand-alone stories.

CHAPTER ONE
Friday Night, Mid-July, The Lounge

Sharlene Michaelsen Boyd checked her watch. 8:23 p.m.

Abso-frickin-tastic.

She'd been back home for less than twenty-four hours and already she wanted to leave Mirabelle Harbor again. Or go to bed earlier than most first graders. Or get really drunk.

At this point, it was a tossup as to which option she'd take.

"Another glass of wine?" Elsie, the sixty-something matron of the Quest singles' group, asked her.

Shar shook her head. "Better not. The jetlag's hitting me pretty hard. I should probably go home."

Elsie looked disappointed but spoke with kind understanding. "I don't blame you. You've been on California time for two weeks. But I'm so glad you came to our gathering tonight and filled us in on Julia and Dane."

"Yes!" Therese, a fellow member of their merry band of locals who were looking for love, added. "To think our dear friend Julia Crane is in *Hollywood* for the whole

1

summer...with her *boyfriend* Dane Tyler! I still can't believe she's been dating a *movie star* for almost a *year*. What a fairy tale come true."

"Yeah," Shar murmured, gathering her things and pulling out some cash to pay her share of the bill. "It was wonderful seeing them both. And Analise, too."

Shar's teaching colleague in the junior high English department and her best friend in all the world—Julia Crane—was a young widow with an eleven-year-old daughter, Analise. When Julia met her teen idol in person for the first time last summer, well, let's just say that sparks flew, and not in a good way. At least not initially.

But that changed and nothing made Shar happier than seeing her BFF in a loving relationship again, albeit a long-distance one. Dane was not only a talented, world-famous actor, he proved to be a warm and thoughtful man. He was good to Julia, and to Analise as well. And he'd been very kind to Shar, too, when she was out in L.A. visiting her friend.

But now Shar was back, and the fairy-tale fantasy that true love was possible—almost easy to believe when in the company of such a happy couple—was wearing off, like body glitter after a hot shower.

"Tell her we said hello," Linda, another of their friends, insisted. "I can't wait to see her again when the school year starts. And say hi to Vicky, too! Just because she's hooked up with your brother now, doesn't mean she can't come out and meet us all for a drink every once in a while."

Shar swallowed away a feeling that was something like envy. "I'll be sure to remind her of that," she said.

But Shar knew high school French teacher Vicky Bernier fairly well, and she knew her older brother Blake even better. Much as she loved them both, trying to pry the two of them apart for an evening was damned near impossible nowadays.

Blake, a local DJ at 102.5 "LOVE" FM, had finally

seen the point of "those silly love songs" he spun on the radio once he and Vicky had gotten together last fall. The two of them were in serious planning mode for a trip they wanted to take to Paris this summer, so they were spending every free moment they had Googling landmarks and booking tours. Trying to have a conversation with either of them was like talking to a human edition of Fodor's *France*.

Although Shar liked everyone in the Quest group, even the currently unattached thirty- or forty-something men who made up almost half of the club members, she didn't want to date any of them. Honestly, there wasn't even one she'd consider bringing back to her condo for a mindless one-night stand. And that was just sad.

By this stage in her life, she should've been able to get over her cheating ex-husband, Stephen "The Snake" Boyd. But she hadn't. She should've been willing to try dating again, even if she was way too apprehensive to get married a second time. Finding just the right man for a casual relationship was harder than it seemed in the movies. Which sucked.

And this meant she'd have to go home and have another lonely night by herself, with only her TV remote for company.

She said goodbye to her friends and stepped out into Harbor Square, the heart of her hometown. She'd walked the few blocks from her condo to the wine bar and had to hoof it back through the muggy midsummer air to get home. She didn't mind the hike, but the emptiness that awaited...

No.

She wasn't ready for that. Not tonight.

Next door to The Lounge was Max's Pub, an institution in Mirabelle Harbor. Unlike the fancy and fairly new wine bar frequented by many of her single friends, Max's had been around for decades. It'd been a regular haunt of

Blake's before he became a monogamous man, and it had the reputation of being an excellent pickup spot.

She slipped inside.

Shar knew it was unlikely that she'd meet anyone new or interesting here either, but the several glasses of white wine she'd downed at The Lounge made her bold. That and the fact that she was wearing skin-tight jeans, spiked black leather boots, and a hot-pink blouse, which she knew emphasized her chest. Why the hell not at least give it a try, right?

She made an effort to glide gracefully over to the bar and was gratified to see a few male heads turn. Not her type, not any of them, but maybe that'd change in an hour or two. At least she could stave off the loneliness for a little longer by being here.

She ordered a strawberry margarita from Gina, one of the regular bartenders, and glanced around the crowded room. Damn. There was no one who caught her eye. No one who was hot enough to raise the tiny hairs on her forearms. No one who could make her believe in the fantasy of a good man—not even until morning.

But, hey, the music was decent—Fall Out Boy was blaring through the speakers overhead, and she liked them—the margarita was strong, and at the other end of the bar, almost hidden in shadow, sat one of her brother Blake's longtime pals, Declan Night.

Shar took back her thoughts about no one in the bar being hot.

Dec qualified. Big time.

From a purely objective standpoint, the man was a pleasure to look at. She'd always thought so. From the top of his dark head to the tip of his sneaker toe, he was all muscle, intensity, and faded denim. But he might as well have been a monk who'd made a vow of celibacy for all Shar cared.

First and foremost, he was a friend of her brother's, and

that put him squarely into the No Touch Zone.

And, secondly, the former hockey player turned sportswriter and business owner was a bigger manwhore than even Blake used to be. And he was a *jock*, heaven forbid. Not that she didn't like sports or that she thought he was totally witless or anything, but she was a self-respecting English teacher and didn't want to talk about slapshots or new draft picks all evening.

Then again, it was summer vacation. She didn't want to discuss *Silas Marner* or *Lord of the Flies* either. Maybe a little hockey talk would distract her.

She picked up her drink and strolled over to where he was sitting, sliding onto the stool next to his. Declan Night, a man who usually gave off the air of being King of the World, was staring deeply into his golden whiskey, like he was a fortuneteller and the glass was his crystal ball.

"Hey, Dec. How are you doing?"

He glanced at her and shrugged. "Life sucks, Shar."

Yeah, well, she wasn't going to argue with him on that. "I know."

He lifted his whiskey and she raised her margarita and they clinked. Then he swallowed every drop of his drink and waved Gina over.

He pointed to Shar's half-empty margarita glass. "Want another of those or you want to try a grown-up beverage?"

Shar studied the ice chips left at the bottom of his whiskey glass. "Your grown-up drink sounds good to me, but I want the happy syrup in mine, instead of whatever she added to yours."

This earned her a lazy half grin from Dec and a laugh from Gina.

"Two whiskey sours," he said to Gina. "But give Shar all of my maraschino cherries and maybe a little extra cherry juice, okay? She wants *happy* syrup."

"Sure thing," the bartender said, smiling. She brought over the drinks immediately, and Dec handed her a large bill.

"Oh, here," Shar said, opening her purse. "Let me give you—"

"Nah, it's on me," he told her. "You already cheered me up a bit. I'm grateful."

"So, what's wrong in your world?" Shar asked once Gina had moved out of earshot. "Why does life suck? Not that I don't have my own reasons for believing that, too..."

He raised a dark eyebrow. "I'll share if you'll share."

She nodded.

"Alrighty, then." He took a deep breath. "What's *wrong* is that my friends keep getting attached to women in a serious way. Geoff Everett has been with Kelsie for, like, two years. He's still a photographer for the *Mirabelle Harbor Gazette*, so I see him around the paper's office and during the occasional interview, but we rarely hang out anymore. Just a few weeks ago, our good buddy, Trevor Cayne, was driving to Colorado Springs to work on a story, and he meets this Tina Marie Moran chick in the middle of Nebraska. An aspiring country music singer who was heading out to Tennessee to try to land a recording deal. And now Trev's gone and *moved to Nashville* to be with her. It's insane."

"Oh, yeah. Blake mentioned something about that," Shar said. "A new redhead in Trev's life, right? Weren't the two of them in town recently?"

He nodded bleakly. "Yep. She's sweet and everything, but all the frickin' way to *Tennessee?* He's eight hours away from us now." Dec glared at his glass and took a long swig. "And don't get me started on your damn brother and his little *mademoiselle*."

"Tell me about it," she commiserated. "It used to be a pain to try to get him to a Michaelsen family gathering *before*—and he was never on time even then—but *now*, forget it. If I don't make the arrangements with Vicky directly, Blake would never show up for anything. And I miss the girls' nights out I used to have with Vicky and our friend Julia, too. I know they've both been juggling a lot this year with work commitments and their boyfriends and—"

"It's just a bunch of BS," he ranted. "All of our friends are crazy to keep these long-term, super-serious relationships going. Moving out of state, even. For 'love'?" He used air quotes. "It's lunacy."

Shar thought about Julia again. Although her best friend technically still lived in Mirabelle Harbor, she and her daughter spent so much time in L.A. with Dane, or she was so preoccupied when he was here, or she was working late at the school to finish up lesson plans so she could take time off to fly to one of Dane's premieres or something—not that this wasn't totally understandable—but there just wasn't as much time for a ladies-only lunch or evening out. Shar knew Julia made as much time for her as she could, and it was wonderful getting to chat with her again and laugh together out in California these past couple of weeks, but that didn't keep Shar from missing her BFF during the many weeks before and after.

A few days ago, when she'd worriedly asked Julia if she was planning to move out to L.A.—given all the air miles the happy couple had been racking up from their cross-country flights—her friend didn't say no. She said, "Not yet."

"What's keeping you from doing that, girlfriend?" Shar had asked, trying to be encouraging of whatever choices her friend decided to make.

"I love Mirabelle Harbor," Julia had said. "It's home, and I don't want to relocate Analise just yet. Her father's grave is there, and I love our house and enjoy my job. And Dane grew up in the Chicago area and will most likely do some occasional theater in the city, like he did last summer." Dane was the headlining actor in a lighthearted play that ran in Chicago, which was how he and Julia met.

"But mostly I'd miss my friends. Like *you*." She hugged her then, and Shar knew Julia was being sincere, but she suspected it was only a matter of time before Julia reconsidered the living arrangements. And the loss Shar would feel then would be as heavy as Declan's in missing his buddy Trevor.

"Yeah," Shar said to Dec. "I love my friends, and I miss them like crazy right now. But what can we do? They're making the choices they want to make, yes?"

Dec sighed and ordered them another round of whiskeys, which they drank in companionable silence. And then *another* round, where they got a little chattier.

Shar had to admit, his "grown-up drink" was relaxing her body and numbing her mind. "I think it would be so much easier if people could just sleep together and forget about all the domestic sharing stuff," she said. It'd been over five years since her divorce, and she wasn't anxious to ever return to a marriage state. But a Friends with Benefits arrangement? *That* she could work with, depending on how sane the man in question was.

"Yes," Dec said, nodding slowly. "They'd just agree with each other that sex is a natural need and a good, healthy aerobic activity, but that doing it didn't require moving in together, spending every waking moment in each other's company, being introduced to the other person's family or—God forbid—exchanging wedding rings in front of a hundred witnesses."

She laughed. Declan Night was, perhaps, smarter than she'd thought. "Agreed. Although there are a number of religions worldwide that would be strongly opposed to this idea."

He shrugged. "You know what I mean, though."

She did.

She studied Dec's handsome face, chiseled jaw, deep brown eyes, five o'clock shadow, and a great many of the muscles he'd acquired from a lifetime of fitness, and Shar concluded that he wasn't only more intelligent than she'd given him credit for, he was also even sexier.

Like her kid brother, Chance, who was a personal trainer and worked out every day without fail, Dec had one of those torsos where his athletic build couldn't be disguised. Not even by the black leather jacket he was wearing or the way he was hunched over the bar.

Unlike her kid brother, Chance, however, she suddenly had an unnerving desire to stroke Dec's chest with her fingertips, say inappropriate things in his ear, and do raunchy stuff with him in an empty locker room. Where had that impulse originated?

She stared at her drink suspiciously. People weren't supposed to mix their alcohols, she remembered too late. She shrugged, fished out one of the whiskeyed cherries, and popped it into her mouth. Mmm. A burst of sweetness with a sharp bite behind it. She liked that combo.

She smiled as she chewed, and Dec looked over at her, watching her lips.

She reminded herself once more that he and Blake were longtime friends. That Dec was strictly off limits.

Then again, he was still staring at her, and his gaze had slipped from her mouth to her chest to her legs...and then back up again to her face. He met her eye and watched some more. Waiting. But for what?

The only excuse she could give for what she said next was that she'd had half a bottle of wine at The Lounge, one jumbo margarita and three whiskey sours here at Max's, and she hadn't gotten laid in more months than she could count. Her ability to think straight was definitely impaired and her willingness to filter her thoughts was even more limited.

"What's stopping us from sleeping together?" she asked him. "I mean, Dec—" She glanced around the room. "Aside from you, there's no one here that I'd want to pick up. You're hotter than anyone else in the bar. It's only because of Blake that I wouldn't flirt with you."

"Same here!" Dec banged the bar counter with his fist for emphasis, making their drink glasses rattle. "I would've hit on you in a heartbeat, Shar," he sort of slurred. "Because you're a seriously sexy woman. But Blake—man, he'd have my head. He told me, like four or five years ago, that he'd kick my ass if I touched you or even looked at you funny. And I believed him. So that was that. I mean—"

"Wait. Blake told you not to go near me? Not to *touch* me?"

"Damn right he did. Why do you think I never flirted with you? I'd already lost a couple of teeth in hockey games. I didn't wanna lose any more. Besides, I remember when you were married to that cheating scumbag and your brother practically disemboweled the guy when he found out—"

"He told you about Stephen's affair?"

Dec winced. "I kinda already knew. Sorry, Shar. Mirabelle Harbor's a small town, you know."

Yeah. She knew.

Shar sighed. Then she replayed Dec's comments in her, admittedly, fuzzy brain. "Well, you're not like my dickhead ex-husband. Blake's interference when it comes to *you* is ridiculous," she said, feeling the full force of indignation hitting her hard. "We can make out or hook up if we want to and not be stupid about it or get overly attached or anything." A statement that seemed to make perfect sense after multiple drinks and very few hours of sleep. "Blake can't tell us what to do. Besides, he's *wrong*. Just because he got his emotions all tangled up with Vicky, it doesn't mean we'll do the same."

"I know, right? The sheer illogic of it! You should've heard Trevor yakking on and on about Tina Marie *this* and Tina Marie *that*. He's just as bad as your brother. Even worse. Trev lost, like, half his vocabulary in the week after he met her. All he could say to defend himself was crazy shit like, 'It just feels right when I'm with her' and crap like that." He rolled his eyes. "And now he's probably changed team allegiances, too, and is cheering for the Nashville Predators instead of the Chicago Blackhawks. I just—just don't even *recognize* him anymore."

"They have no self control." Shar rested the flat of her palm on Dec's hard chest. "Mmm, very nice," she told him. "But see? I could totally resist you tomorrow." And, to demonstrate, she pulled her hand away and shrugged like it was no biggie. Weird, though, that her palm turned a little sweaty just from that brief touch... Huh. She'd ignore that.

"Of course you could," Dec agreed, slowly fingering a lock of Shar's long hair. "And I could resist you, too." He suddenly flicked away one of her ringlets. "These friends in our lives are like teenagers who're having their first high school crush or something. No bad relationship experiences. No real perspective. Not like *us*."

She nodded, recalling her brother telling her about Dec's former fiancée—a nightmare—Trisha something-or-other. How their argumentative, rocky engagement hadn't even lasted six months. Shar and her ex had at least faked being a happily married couple for two years.

"They're weaklings," she concluded. "They don't know how to set limits." Although, even with the strange mist rolling around in her head, Shar didn't entirely believe her own words. She was thinking about her former self more than about her closest friends and their behavior. She'd made too many damn mistakes in the past with boundaries. She wouldn't let that happen again.

"We should show 'em how it's done," Dec suggested.

"Yeah," she said.

"Yeah," he said back. Then he studied the almost empty whiskey glass in his hand, set it down, and eyed her warily. "Sharlene, do you really mean that?"

She considered the question. Even with the many drinks, her brain all foggy, and the jetlag-induced sleep deprivation, she *did* mean it.

She nodded. "I do." Then she laughed. "That's the closest I've gotten to ever saying those words again."

He laughed with her, if a bit more ruefully. "Hey, you got a helluva lot closer than I did. I couldn't say it even once." He paused. "So, okay." He jumped up from his barstool and tossed some extra bills on the counter for Gina, who was standing a bit closer than Shar had realized and staring at the two of them with a gaze that was a cross between deeply concerned and vaguely horrified.

Uh-oh.

Dec wobbled a little as he stood up. Clearly, he was at least as drunk as she was but, thankfully, he knew it.

"I rode my motorcycle here, but I shouldn't drive it back." He pointed at her. "And you shouldn't drive any kind of vehicle either, so we're gonna have to walk."

"I'd anticipated having a few drinks, so I came on foot to the Square tonight. And I'd already planned to walk home. I'm in the condos on Crescent Lane." Her memory wasn't working all that well at the moment, though. She couldn't recall where Blake had told her Dec's place was. "Um, which one of us lives closer?"

He squinted, deep in thought. "Me, I think. It's a straight shot down Spring Street to Main. My apartment's just above my shop."

"Oh, that's right."

Dec owned The Penalty Box—a sports clothing and memorabilia store in downtown Mirabelle Harbor. She'd never had a reason to go in it, but it was a popular stop for the athletically minded residents in town, and it was located diagonally across the street from The Gala—the Greek restaurant and bakery owned by Chance's girlfriend, Nia Pappyiannis, and her family. It was also just a few doors down from Not the Same Old Grind, the best coffeehouse on the North Shore, in Shar's opinion. So she knew they'd be to his place in less than ten minutes...if they didn't trip, stop, keel over, or otherwise collapse on the sidewalk.

"Your place it is, then," she declared.

"Okay. Let me hit the men's room quick and we can go."

Gina's look of grave concern turned to undisguised alarm at this pronouncement. The moment Dec disappeared from view, the bartender pulled her aside.

"Listen, Shar, I can call you a cab or drive you home myself when my shift ends. This is none of my business and typically I'd stay out of it, but you and Declan have both been drinking more than usual, and I know your brother pretty well. Blake would be *extremely* worried about you if he heard—"

"Which is why you're not gonna tell him, Gina. If this is a mistake, it's gotta be *my* mistake."

"But why risk making a mistake at all?"

"Because I haven't taken *any* relationship risks in years and, really, this isn't much of one either. We're talking a simple one-night stand with no strings attached for either of us. And just *look* at Dec."

Both women watched him as he headed back toward them, weaving his hunky body through the crowded bar, all smoldering, dark, and sinful. Shar's mouth watered in anticipation of kissing him, and her fingers all but twitched with the desire to hold him and squeeze.

"Mmmm," Gina murmured. "Yeah, okay. He's hot. I'll give you that. But—"

"But that's all I'm looking for tonight."

Gina nodded and stepped away, just as Dec reached the counter. He gazed at Shar with a scorching look that made her want to peel off her hot-pink blouse and fan herself.

It'd been a long time since she'd propositioned a guy. This moment should've felt awkward. But it didn't. And when Dec reached for her hand, he did more than take it in his. He pulled her to him and brought his lips down on hers.

Holy shit. The jock could kiss.

A few customers nearby wolf whistled, but none of them were people Shar knew and, anyway, she didn't care. Her lips tingled, and she wanted more. Like, immediately.

"Ready to go?" Dec whispered.

"Yep."

And with a parting wave to a wide-eyed, worried-looking Gina, Shar followed him out of Max's Pub and into the heart of the hot summer night.

CHAPTER TWO
Declan's Apartment

Sharlene Michaelsen Boyd. In his place.

Oooh, baby.

He'd fantasized about this but hadn't dared to imagine it'd ever happen.

Declan said a prayer of thanks to the laundry gods that he'd been inspired to pick up all his shit on the floor yesterday and wash his clothes and sheets. His apartment was absent of his stinky workout shirts, and the pillowcases on his bed still had that fresh-floral detergent scent. He had hopes that his entire place would smell like Shar, though, when the night was over.

He always kept beer and wine on hand, breakfast foods in the fridge, and a mammoth box of condoms in the bedroom drawer. Just because he'd never been a Boy Scout, it didn't mean he wasn't prepared.

Dec watched Shar look around, take in the furniture, the decor, the old hockey trophies, and the awards. She appeared suitably impressed but distracted. He could understand that. It was all he could do not to drag her into his bedroom and start the disrobing process.

"Would you like something to drink?" he asked politely. "Or, um, a snack? I've got—"

She cut him off with a laugh. "Hell, no, Dec. Just kiss me again, like you did at the bar."

He nodded obediently, strode over to her at once, and cradled her face in his palms. Then he brought his lips to meet hers...and *hot damn*.

Pure, burning-red combustion.

It was as if something between the two of them actually ignited, like setting a lit match to a gas burner. Only the flame that sparked when their mouths collided spread instantly through his body, and his internal temperature spiked to scorching levels within seconds.

He checked her up against the living room wall, like he might an opponent in the hockey rink. Unlike when he played the game on the ice, though, he lingered with Shar. He touched her. He had his hands on her tight ass, reducing the space from his chest to hers from twenty millimeters to zero in a split second.

She responded by sliding her fingertips up his back, underneath his T-shirt, against his bare skin. Then, intensifying the friction between them as he arched into her, she raked her nails all the way down from his shoulder blades to his waist. It hurt, but what a fucking turn on.

What could he say? He liked a little pain with his pleasure.

And from the way Shar moaned when he kneaded her flesh through the thin denim and ground her lower body between the wall and his rock-hard erection, she liked it a little rougher, too.

As if confirming this, she nipped his bottom lip when he was kissing her—sharp enough for him to taste the tang of his own blood.

He licked his lips and grinned at her. "Hell, Shar. You're making me wish I still had my handcuffs."

"What? No handcuffs? I'm disappointed." But she carried on, unbuckling his belt, unzipping his jeans, popping a button on his shirt as she tore it off him.

Trish the Tramp, his lying and thieving ex-fiancée, had run off with Dec's satin-lined sex-cuffs when she moved out. She'd taken other things from him, too: his favorite Train CD from one of their earlier concerts, his signed Blackhawks team jersey—just out of spite—and a decent chunk of his self-respect.

"I've got a stash of neckties in the dresser we could knot up, though, if you wanna play bondage games," he told Shar.

She laughed. "I'll keep that in mind for later tonight. Round two. Or three."

Sexy as he already thought she was, her optimism about the direction of the evening made her even more so. He let her push his jeans to the floor then helped her get rid of those black leather boots, hot-pink shirt, and painted-on jeans. Underneath was just wisps of lacy white fabric and smooth creamy skin.

Dec gripped her thigh and ran his thumb just under the lace of her panties, bringing the pads of his fingers closer to her center. To the heat and wetness waiting for him to stroke. On the outside. And the inside.

He knew as soon as he caressed her—as soon as she arched toward him and moaned—that she'd devour him whole tonight. That he was going to lose himself in her. That while he was the one doing most of the physical touching at the moment, not vice versa, he'd end up more affected by their encounter than she would.

I'm so fucked, but I don't care.

There was something about Shar that he both admired and feared. Her toughness. He knew it wasn't just an act. She was fiercely loyal and generous to those she loved. He'd seen her in action with her family and close friends.

But getting invited into her inner circle wasn't an easy

feat. The lady had a well-protected heart, despite this show of intimacy and openness. Despite the alcohol she'd consumed. And despite any words she might utter in passion's wake.

If he'd been looking for a what-you-see-is-what-you-get woman, he'd managed to choose the opposite. Shar would fight hard to keep those walls she'd erected impenetrable and towering.

Still, he was motivated to try to level them. Crush and crumble them under the force of his kisses. A man didn't get to the pros in any sport without a healthy competitive spirit.

"C'mon, Dec," she cried as he teased her clit, first with his fingertips and then with his tongue. "Stop the effing foreplay and *do* me. Jeez."

He chuckled. He didn't usually have a problem with self-control during sex, but damned if he didn't want to be inside her just as much as she seemed to want the same.

"Fine," he said.

He was fighting to keep at least a shred of mental distance as he hauled her into his bedroom, grabbed a fistful of condoms, tore one open, and slid it on. Then, flipping her onto the edge of the bed, face down with her feet on the floor and her stomach on the mattress, he plunged deep into her.

Oh, God. The *feel* of her as he pumped in hard and glided out slow. The rhythm they found and built together within just a few seconds... So. Smokin'. Hot.

"Faster," she told him. "Harder. And stronger. Just like the Olympic motto."

He did his best to comply with her commands, even as he tried not to laugh. He managed to say, "It's *higher,* Shar, not harder. The motto. Not that I care, but—oh, baby! Do that again."

She flexed some muscles deep inside her and squeezed his cock, massaging it. He groaned and felt sweat tracking

18

patterns down his face, his shoulders, his chest. But he pulled her tighter. Pushed deeper. Breathed heavier.

"It's higher, really? Are you sure?"

"I'm sure."

"Well, it shouldn't be," she panted, but he could hear the amusement in her sexy voice.

"Okay. You win," he strained to reply. "I've just decided that the Olympic Committee should change the motto to your version. I'll email them this week with your suggestion."

He had the pleasure of hearing her laugh as she came...and, man, she came hard. Dec's pride in that moment surprised even him. Her lithe body shuddered with near violence beneath him, her fingernails gripped the covers on his bed, and beads of perspiration glistened on her silky back, dampening her long glossy hair, as well as endless, beautiful skin.

A few more strokes and squeezes from her and he came just as hard. Holy mother. That was *fast*.

Then...then he just held her—motionless and mute, except for their ragged breaths, which were synchronized to nearly identical rhythms. The world stopped rotating on its axis. The clock stopped ticking. There was nothing else that existed in space-time but the two of them on the bed together. Sweaty. Silent. Sated.

Dec lost track of how long they stayed like that. Just breathing. But, eventually, he wrenched himself away, just long enough to get rid of the condom, and nestled with her under the covers she'd all but torn off.

"Why didn't we ever do that before?" she whispered.

He brushed a long, dark, wavy tendril away from her forehead and murmured. "Because we were idiots."

She nodded sleepily.

And for a few hours, they slept like the dead.

Shar's palm sliding against his hard-on nudged him awake. Her eyes were still closed, but her hands were feeling him up in the dark, like a horny teenager. Not quite as fast and furious as before. More of an achingly slow and tender ramble. Another mysterious side of Shar.

He let her take the lead this time, dictating the pace. He wondered if she was even aware she was doing it. If, to her, this was all part of some super-sexy dream. Certain people had a habit of sleepwalking. Maybe Shar was prone to sleepfucking?

Her fingers encircled his cock and danced along the ridge until he had to turn his head away, jaw tense, and moan into his pillow. But he didn't still her hand. And he didn't steal the control from her.

"I could've sworn you had enough rubbers in this room for a Roman orgy," she whispered, her eyes still shut, but the knowing smile on her lips made him sure she was fully conscious.

"Maybe. I don't have a definitive head count on that yet. A Roman orgy is still on my bucket list."

"Smart ass," she said. "Hand me one of the extras, will you?"

He felt around the nightstand for a foil packet and did as she asked.

Without so much as a peek at the condom, she ripped open the square packet, sheathed him, and pulled herself on top of his body—taking him in and sinking down in one ultra-smooth motion. Then she rode him like an experienced jockey, but it wasn't as untamed as before. Not like two wild animals meeting and mating in the jungle.

No.

This was slow. And soft. A beguiling nonverbal conversation between their bodies. So tender that he felt an unexpected dampness in the corners of his eyes that didn't come from sweat. *What the hell?*

This, too, was Shar, he reminded himself. She was strong and fierce and protective...but he could also see hints of the sweet gentleness underneath. The sensitivity, vulnerability, and nakedness, which had nothing to do with her clothing—or lack thereof.

Hints of all this, yes. But not the full dosage.

To get that coveted entree into her inner world would take more than a little work. At the very least, he'd have to get her to open her eyes and look at him. Really *see* him.

He swallowed and reached to pull her face down toward his. To entice her to bring her lips to meet his greedy mouth. When finally she did, he kissed her with every ounce of hopefulness he possessed. He bared his soul to her in that second and found himself willing her to be curious enough to gaze into his eyes and see the man beneath her. A man who felt an unfamiliar longing in her presence that he didn't want to admit. To anyone.

But she didn't look.

She pulled away, rode him faster, and watched only the vision behind her closed eyelids.

He pulled her lips to his again, this time tracing intricate patterns on her back and thighs, as he soul-kissed her. He pressed his palms more firmly against her flesh, cradling her body, before using his greater strength to reverse their positions, his mouth never leaving hers.

Then, when she was secure beneath him, he stretched both of her hands up to the pillow above her head—rubbing her soft fingers with his callused ones—and grasping them like faux handcuffs, while his hips pumped slowly forward and back. While their tongues tangled in a game of give and take.

It almost killed him to stop, but she was stubbornly persistent in paying more attention to the man in her head than to the man making love to her. He hoped like hell those images were one and the same.

"Dec?" She tried to motion him into moving again by wiggling and straining against the bonds he'd created, but he could be stubborn, too. He'd let her have her way before, but she wasn't going to win *this* round.

"Look at me, Shar."

"But I'm tired, and it's dark in here."

He smiled. "Not so dark with the moonlight streaming in. Open your eyes and see for yourself."

Reluctantly, she propped open one heavy lid, resembling for a second an absolutely gorgeous lady pirate. Then she cracked open the other eye and glanced around. "You're right. It's not too dark. It's too bright." And she firmly shut her eyes again.

"Oh, no, you don't." He kissed each eyelid. Then he waited with grueling patience, holding himself completely still above her while she pushed against both of his hands and slammed her hips upward toward him.

He didn't budge.

She puffed out in frustration, "Damn you, Declan!"

"Sharlene, c'mon. I'm not that scary up close, am I?" he whispered. "I want to see the rings of your irises when you come this time. Please. Look at me."

Eyes still shut, she frowned. "Why?"

"Because...even though we're doing this just for tonight, I want to see every part of you. I want to know you. And—" Shit. He couldn't believe he was gonna say this aloud, but Shar did strange things to him. "I want you to know me, too."

Damned if it wasn't the truth.

"Really?"

"Yes."

Even in the shadow of his darkened bedroom, the stunning blue of her eyes glittered when she opened them up for him. This time, her gaze fixed steadily and intently on his, so much so that he nearly had to look away himself. But he didn't.

He swallowed. "Thank you."

And then he kissed her lips and began to make love to her again in earnest. He pulled his face back just far enough to keep the connection of their gazes intact as he moved slowly and deeply inside of her. She whimpered a few times and bit her lip to stop, but she didn't close her eyes. Not more than a blink or two, anyway. And she didn't speak either, just moved very tenderly, in waves along with him, as he quickened the pace and brought her to the point where she was breathless and gasping.

The expression in her eyes—because he sure as hell wasn't going to stop watching them—somehow managed to be both hotly passionate and coolly perplexed, even as she came apart in his arms. It was only once he could feel her body relax that he let himself come, too. And her gaze was trained on him every second.

Oh, God, oh, God, oh, God.

Even though he'd been the one to insist on eye contact, he barely learned anything more about her. He, on the other hand, had just offered up his soul to her as she stared back at him. Fuck.

Dec closed his eyes.

He slid to the mattress, his breathing ragged—not just from physical excursion but also because of a new, strange anxiety gripping his chest.

Shar didn't speak. Didn't ask any questions or chide him for being the first to look away. Nope. She just snuggled up against him like a baby bunny and fell back asleep.

He couldn't sleep for shit. His mind just raced.

This was a freakin' *one-night stand*. There was *no* pressure. *No* commitment. Just *mutual* agreement. Why was he feeling so...nervous...or whatever this was? It reminded him of that painful flash of performance anxiety he'd felt in the rink, after he'd been benched for a few weeks because of a knee injury. The fear that he might screw up royally hadn't lasted long, but it was agonizing for those brief minutes.

The difference between then and now was that, back then, the feeling had dissipated midway through the first period. Here, more than an hour had gone by, and all the tensions within him had only tightened and grown.

Dec finally caught a bit of shuteye, but the light from his window was increasingly bright and persistent. The summer sun wanted to burn a hole through his skin, and it wasn't even eight a.m.

Shar rolled away from him and mumbled something unintelligible.

In spite of himself, he laughed. She was so damned cute in the morning. At any time of day, really.

"Want some breakfast?" he asked her.

She wrinkled her nose and squinted at him. "Tell me you have coffee. Very strong coffee."

"I have very strong coffee and will make you a large pot of it. Any other requests?"

Her eyes opened a bit wider, and she raised both delicately arched eyebrows as she scanned his naked torso with a lascivious glance. "We're just talking about *food,* right?"

"Not necessarily." Although his stomach rumbled, he was more than willing to ignore his body's hunger pangs, especially if it meant getting in round three with Shar before breakfast.

"You know how jam is usually served on toast?"

He nodded.

"I don't need the toast if you're in here with me. Just the jar. And maybe a spoon—for spreading."

Or maybe round three *was* breakfast.

He grinned at her. Then he went into the kitchen, set up the coffee maker, and pulled out a jar of orange marmalade from the fridge. He also grabbed a spoon and returned to the bedroom, handing both of these items over to her.

"I'm at your mercy, sweetheart." He said this jokingly, but the way his heart was hammering inside his chest spoke to the honesty of his words. He didn't want to like her this much...and prayed she'd be gentle with him.

Shar studied the marmalade thoughtfully before dipping the spoon into the jar and giving it a taste. "Mmm. Sweet. Tangy. A little unexpected. I took you for more of a traditional strawberry or grape guy. You've astonished me, Dec. Imported English marmalade is surprisingly posh."

"What can I say? I'm a man of hidden depth."

She laughed, like the chiming of little golden bells. "We're going to have fun with this," she promised, setting the jar down carefully on the nightstand. "But—"

"But what?"

"Can I ask you a question?"

Oh, crap. That's rarely good. "Uh, sure."

She licked her lips and a bolt of red-hot arousal went straight from his eyes to his dick. How the hell had she managed to get under his skin this fast? He was terrified to let himself fall completely under her spell, but he didn't want to be even half a room away from her. Seriously. What was wrong with him?

He slid back into the bed, next to her once again. The warmth of her body heating the air temperature in the room like it was some kind of sweat lodge.

"Why isn't this more awkward?" She motioned between the two of them with her index finger. "I mean, I've had a few embarrassing morning afters in my life, and I'm guessing you've scored in the—what—upper two digits? Or the lower threes, right?"

She paused, and he thought back to the years of bar hookups, after-game one-night stands with hockey groupies, babes he'd met at his teammates' house parties...whose last names he'd never known. (And more than a few first names he'd forgotten.) So many fuzzy and forgettable sexcapades. Almost all of them seemed ridiculous or pointless from his current vantage point.

"Yep." He shrugged. "But this—" He mimed the same action with his index finger, motioning between them. "This isn't exactly the same thing, Shar. We're not strangers to each other. And we're both people of our word. We *said* we were gonna do this and we *did*. No clinginess. No strings. No relationship pressure—"

"No domestic crap. No talk of falling in love or moving in together," she concluded.

"And that's why it's not so awkward," he said. Though it kind of was, wasn't it? Just not in the way he was used to. "We're good at this, Shar. At keeping it real. No games. No drama. No uncomfortable silences." *Just my body having a near panic attack over getting to spend the whole night with you...*

She sighed. "I wish there were more men out there like you, Dec. So reasonable."

"Or like you. Honestly, I don't know any women who are half as sane as you are. Sexy as fuck, but not, like, planning our engagement after one hot night."

She bobbed her head and fingered the spoon for the jam. "It's almost too bad that we promised each other it would be for one night only. I'm not going to feel this comfortable with the next guy I pick up."

Something bitter and distasteful lodged itself in his throat as he listened to her saying this. Sharlene. Picking up another guy at Max's Pub. Or anywhere, really... Shit.

He took a deep breath and tried to keep his tone even as he spoke. "Look, don't feel like you have to write me off just because we had our one-night stand already. We can do it again...*anytime*. And it can still be just as string-free as last night."

She appeared to be considering this. "Yeah, I mean, I guess as long as we don't get too, um, consistent or anything, it'll be fine. I'm still totally able to resist you."

He forced a laugh. "Same here," he insisted, although a small part of his brain screamed that he was a damned liar. Weird thing was, the tightening in his gut eased up a bit at the thought that, maybe, this conversation might lead to them spending another night together. Sometime. Maybe even soonish. He didn't want to analyze why that would make him feel *better,* not more trapped.

"Good." Shar motioned him closer with the tip of the spoon, which she'd just dipped into the jar. A couple drops of marmalade dripped onto her beautiful chest.

He leaned in, counting the seconds until he could lick them off of her. She dangled the sweet spoonful in the air, as if trying to decide where she should spread it first—on him or on herself.

Before she made her choice, though, he had a question of his own.

"You got any plans for tonight?" he asked.

She shook her head, her long dark hair brushing her shoulders.

He wove his fingers through the tangled strands and gently brought her to him. But before his lips could come into contact with her skin, and before he was going to let her have her way with the spoon and the jar of sweet orange stickiness, he was going to nail down the exact details of the night ahead.

"So, what do you say about dinner tonight? Seven p.m., maybe?"

"Sure."

Then he watched—and felt the result—as she turned the spoon toward him and slingshotted the marmalade, Jackson Pollock-style, at his torso. She grinned deviously at him and, man, he was such a goner. He wanted to touch her again so bad it hurt. Being with her was like Nirvana, the Stanley Cup Finals, and the Food Network all rolled into one.

"Uh, my apartment or do you wanna go out on the town?" he managed to ask.

"Neither," she said. "Come to my place. You bring the food. I'll have the drinks."

"Deal."

"Oh, and—" Shar paused to fill another spoonful and

splatter it on him again. She seemed to enjoy this form of art design. "I'll have the handcuffs, too."

.

CHAPTER THREE
Saturday, 11:03 a.m.

Freshly showered and a little unstable on her feet (not from last night's drinking, but just from so many hours in Dec's bed), Shar let him give her a lift to her condo in his sporty blue convertible.

"See you in about eight hours," he said with a grin so steamy it gave her skin a heat rash. "Any cuisine requests for dinner? Italian? All-American? Thai?"

"Nope. You can surprise me. Just, um—maybe, you might want to steer clear of anywhere Blake and Vicky might go."

He nodded. "Good point. No Sloppy Joe's carryout tonight then, huh?"

"Sadly, no." Sloppy Joe's was one of her brother's favorite haunts and a well-known Mirabelle Harbor establishment. They made the best burgers and fries around.

"I'll avoid it. Though Blake's probably too preoccupied with other things to think about either of us this weekend," Dec said before he drove off.

Shar wished she could believe that, but she *knew* her brother. Blake had an uncanny, sixth-sense sort of thing when it came to people close to him. He wasn't someone she should see face to face in the next forty-eight hours. Not if she wanted to keep her secrets.

She entered her condo and wandered around like a zombie for more time than she wanted to admit. What had just happened between her and Declan?

It was good sex, sure. *Great* sex, even. And anything that pushed the painful memories of her ex-husband out of her head and buffered her from loneliness for a few hours was a welcome distraction.

Maybe she was just justifying her behavior, but last night had been exactly what she'd been looking for. A classic one-night stand. Although, it seemed to be lasting a little longer than expected.

Never mind. It'd be done by the end of the weekend regardless. Long-term, Cinderella-like love stories were for her friends. Julia had ended up with a *movie star,* for heaven's sake. How often did that happen? And Vicky made her brother a happier and better man. Shar was so damned thrilled for them all, but she knew she was much more cynical than her friends.

And that was what was so perfect about someone like Dec. He wasn't trying to flatter her or fool her. The guy's personal life was a total train wreck, and he was *so not* the kind of man she could ever settle down with, even if she decided to take the serious relationship plunge again. He was a jock who drove hot cars and fast motorcycles. Aside from the weird thing he had about eye contact, he scarcely had a sensitive bone in his body. He was hard everywhere. *Everywhere.* She was pretty sure he was too straightforward to cheat on her, though, and there was hardly enough time for him to do that anyway—at least not in the next day or two. And, best of all, he felt exactly the same way she did about no commitments.

It was an ideal hookup.

But, without a doubt, it was preferable to keep whatever they were doing from Blake. He could be overly protective of his family.

Speaking of family, Shar checked her landline and saw that her sister-in-law, Olivia, had tried to call this morning when she wasn't at home. Odd. Usually, big brother Derek's wife would call her cell instead...

She pulled out her smartphone and, yes, Olivia had called there, too, but Shar had muted the phone last night. Oops.

Three missed calls and seven texts.

She tried to swallow away the panic that rose at seeing this. What if something bad had happened to someone she loved?

Shar quickly listened to the voicemail messages and was, almost immediately, put at ease. Olivia's tone was upbeat. "Hey, just checking in!" and a few other cheery lines. Typically, Olivia and Derek had rather active weekends, especially with their three school-aged sons, all of whom were involved in some sport or other. Olivia had probably called from the sidelines of the soccer field where one of her kids was playing. In any case, a response could wait until later this afternoon, or even tomorrow.

The second message was even less important. Just one of the English curriculum committee members suggesting that the team have a meeting in mid-August before the new school year was set to begin. "Let's run through each of the major curricular changes all together," Meg, one of the most fastidious teachers on the planet, enthused. Shar would deal with scheduling *that* fun gathering later.

The final message (and, as it turned out, all seven texts) were from Julia. "Call me!" her BFF demanded, in both mediums. So Shar didn't waste a second.

"What's going on out there?" Shar asked. It was two hours earlier in California than it was in Mirabelle Harbor.

Just after nine a.m. where Julia was this morning. "Is everything okay?"

"No!" her friend said, but there was laughter in her voice. "I miss you. I was spoiled having you out here with me for two weeks. I love Dane, but he's got a ton of acting responsibilities, and Analise is still spending most of her time with that girl from the neighboring estate. The two of them spend hours swimming and painting their nails and singing this dreadful teeny-bop karaoke. I miss hanging out with my best girlfriend and chatting, too."

"What? You don't miss my karaoke?"

Julia laughed. "Maybe we just need to practice. Vicky's a pretty good singer—at least in the car with the radio on. The three of us need to go out when I get back home. Drink some wine at my house and then crank up the tunes."

Shar grinned. "I like that idea."

"Okay, so now that I've interrupted you in the middle of your morning, fill me in on what's going on in Mirabelle Harbor in the two days since you've been back. How's everybody in the Quest group? Weren't you going out with them last night?"

"Um, yeah." Shar paused. "They're good."

"What's *that* tone mean?"

"What, uh, tone?"

"Seriously, Shar? It's *me* you're talking to. I may be in another time zone, but there's nothing wrong with my hearing. First, it takes you forever to answer my texts, and now you're being evasive. There's something going on with you."

Shar winced. "Okay, look. I was going to tell you about this later, girlfriend, just as soon as it had all played out. But I'm still kind of in the middle of it."

"In the middle of what, exactly? And does it involve a guy?"

"A one-night stand that's actually turning into two nights, I think. And...yes."

Julia squealed loudly enough that Shar had to pull the cell phone away from her ear. "Which man? Do I know him? Tell me everything!"

"After spending a couple of hours at The Lounge with the Quest gang, who miss you terribly, by the way, I wandered over to Max's. And, um, Declan Night was there."

"The guy who owns The Penalty Box? Big, hunky hockey guy?"

"Yep."

Julia squealed again. "Oh, Shar! Was it good?"

"Yes. Understatement."

"Was he nice to you?"

Shar thought about some of the rougher moves Dec used on her last night and couldn't help but grin. "Well, I'm not sure *nice* is the right word for what he was doin—"

"You know what I mean."

"Yeah, I do. And, yes, he was good to me. We're having dinner tonight. Here." And, hopefully, several more hours of raunchy fun.

"That sounds pretty promising—if you want to see him again. Even just for 'dinner,' as you euphemistically call it."

Shar laughed. "It is, as I already said to you, girlfriend, just a fling. You know I don't do long-term relationships. Not anymore."

"Say what you will, but—"

"But what?"

There was a longish, thoughtful pause. "Remember last summer? We had a conversation on the Fourth of July about being ready to find love again," Julia said. "You told me it would be harder for you because you'd been burned so badly with Stephen. That you didn't believe in fantasies like love anymore."

Shar definitely remembered that talk.

"Well, this takes the pressure off. You've got clear

vision. You don't have to worry about big commitments. Just have fun with Declan, even if it lasts longer than a night or two. See if he can help you recover that sense of magic so, maybe, you'll be open to finding your real soulmate sometime."

"Guess you're right. There's nothing to freak out about with Dec. It's just great sex. Really great sex."

Shar heard smothered laughter on the other end of the line. "Exactly," Julia said. "It's not like *that's* any big deal."

She knew her friend's sarcasm when she heard it. Time to change the subject before it got too embarrassing. "So, where's Dane?" Shar asked.

"Showering."

"Without you?"

Julia gave a mock sigh. "This time, yes. He's got an interview at the studio for *The Scorpius Project*, which is coming out in November. He's doing a magazine spread with the rest of the cast, so he has to go in early for hair and makeup. It's crazy. The promo stuff is already exhausting and it's only July. It's going to be nonstop during the release month."

"And he's also filming that other movie, right? The murder mystery one?"

"*Private Eyes*, yes. It's in pre-production," Julia said. "They start shooting next month, which was why Analise and I wanted to be out here beforehand. Once that begins, we'll have even less time with Dane. The good news is that, after today's photo shoot, he's got the rest of the weekend off, so we have plans to visit a vineyard and take Analise out for pizza and canolis. Dane knows this hideaway Italian joint—"

"Enough, enough! Dane and his off-the-beaten-path bakeries and diners." She laughed. "I swear I gained five pounds when I was staying with you guys. Where does he even hear about these little places?"

"I don't know, Shar. The man's got mad skills."

Shar smiled. She didn't need further proof that her BFF's fairytale love story was still going strong. After being in L.A. and watching all of the little ways the two of them showed they cared about and respected each other, she knew this had the makings of a lifetime love.

But there was still that long-distance issue, and whenever she hinted to Julia that she'd have to resolve it at some point, her friend just shrugged. She decided to be more direct this time. "So...any chance he'll pop the question in, say, the next six months or year?"

"He already did."

"What?!"

"Don't get all excited. I mean, Dane and I have talked about it a few times, Shar. It's not like the subject hasn't come up, and half the tabloid articles about us say we've been secretly hitched for months." She laughed.

"But—but you didn't tell *me* that he'd asked you." This was a surprisingly hurtful realization.

"Oh, Shar, do you really think I'd seriously entertain *any* marriage plans without asking you to be my maid of honor? Trust me on this, if or when Dane and I decide to make it official, you'll be the first to know, after my daughter."

This made her feel a bit better. Okay, a *lot* better. "Promise?"

"Yes. Now stop fixating about my love life and get back to yours."

"Whose love life?" Shar heard Dane say to Julia in the background.

"Shar's, but you're not getting involved," Julia replied.

The actor snorted. He must have pulled the phone away from her friend because the next thing Shar heard was Dane's voice through the receiver, with a fake Viennese therapist accent, taking over the conversation. "*Zeet* down on *zee* sofa," he said. "And let's talk about your first *zexual* experience."

"Out of the room, Dane Tyler!" Julia demanded, laughing. Then, to Shar, "Sorry. He's so nosy."

"Oh, I know," she replied. Dane was a master of social media and was always looking up stuff about other people online. The big international movie star had even Googled Julia before they started dating. "But here's how Dane can help. Tell him to do a search on Declan Night. Then he can give me all the advice he wants."

"Done. But until then, you just listen to me," Julia said, her tone light but somehow more serious than Shar would've expected. "Declan is lucky to have you in his life. Whether it's for a few days or for longer. You don't have to please him—or anyone, for that matter. If you get even a hint that he's a bad seed like your ex, you kick his ass to the curb. You hear me?"

"I hear you."

After hanging up the phone, Shar began frantically cleaning her place. Blake called. In fact, he'd called multiple times. Her phone had been beeping while she was talking with Julia, but she didn't want to hang up on her best friend until she was good and ready.

Besides, to be entirely truthful, she was really afraid to talk with her altogether too insightful and perceptive brother.

Last time they'd chatted, he was so excited about this Paris trip with Vicky that he could hardly contain himself.

"Goodness, Blake. You're more wound up than Winston," she said, referring to the cute fluff ball he called a dog.

"He's gonna be in doggie heaven when we're abroad," her brother said, and Shar knew why. Winston would be spending those ten days at the big Michaelsen family home on the lake, along with Derek, Olivia, their three sons, and a big yard full of squirrels.

"Il sera heureux comme un concombre," Blake stated.

She squinted in confusion. "I don't speak French nearly as fluently as your girlfriend, but didn't you just say 'He'll be happy like a cucumber'?"

"Hmm. I might need to work on that expression," Blake admitted. "Good thing Vicky is gonna do most of the talking while we're in Paris."

"Yeah, good thing," she said and listened to him prattle on for another twenty minutes about French phrases he thought would be useful.

"A quelle heure commence le spectacle?"

"Où est la tour Eiffel?"

"Je voudrais le crêpe nutella, s'il vous plaît."

And on and on...

But that was days ago and, since she'd returned from California, she'd only texted her brother once—a courtesy message sent to all her siblings, saying she'd gotten back safely.

This morning, however, he'd made a nuisance of himself by not only calling but, also, texting and asking her things like "Where are you?" and "Whatcha doing?"

Shar rolled her eyes. Then she listened to the voicemail he'd left on his third call attempt.

"Hey, Sis. If I didn't know better, I'd think you were ignoring me. Since when don't you answer your phone or return your text messages, huh? Call me back...or I may have to stop over for an impromptu visit, just to make sure my favorite and only sister is still breathing. Okay?"

He'd chuckled on the line, as if he were being casual and jokey, but there was no mistaking the not-so-thinly-veiled warning in his tone.

She waited only about three minutes before calling him back. "I didn't hear the phone. I was vacuuming and then talking to Julia," she told him, mostly truthfully. "What's up?"

"I had a very interesting conversation with Gina, my favorite bartender, at the Mirabelle Market this morning. She pretended not to see me at first, which was odd behavior." He paused and cleared his throat. "But when I cornered her by the canned peaches, she couldn't get away. Can you guess what we were discussing?"

Oh, shit.

"Uh, no. Not...really." Shar battled the twist of nervousness in the pit of her stomach. "But, um, Gina was probably just tired. She often works late."

"Yeah, that's what she said. But then I asked her if her bar patrons had been behaving themselves, and she got all weird on me. Instead of answering with a simple 'Yes' or 'No,' she said, 'Why?' And then she scurried away real fast. It took me a while before I could find someone I knew who'd been at Max's last night. Someone who said they saw you and Declan there together."

Damn Blake and his popularity in town.

"Oh!" Shar faked a laugh. "That's not quite true. We weren't there together. We just, uh, ran into each other at Max's. I was actually at a Quest gathering at The Lounge last night and was only chatting with Dec for a little while afterward."

"Is that so?" Her brother's disbelief was audible, and Shar remembered too late that there had been that kiss at the bar before she and Dec had left. Together.

Who the hell had been spying on her? And had whomever it was seen that kiss? Not that it wasn't her own fault that she'd been spotted. Neither she nor Dec had been remotely discreet, but she always underestimated the number of people her four brothers knew in Mirabelle Harbor.

"Yes, of course." Then, trying to redirect Blake, "You know, everyone in the Quest group really missed Vicky last night. She used to come to most of our gatherings. Is she there with you?"

"Yeah," he said, all wariness and suspicion.

"Great! Let me say hi to her. I want to tell her about the gang and let her know when the next meet up will be. Plus, I haven't talked with her since I got back from L.A., and I have a few messages for her from Julia."

"Look, Shar, it's not that I don't want you to talk with my girlfriend. It's just that I finally got ahold of you and, if you're in any way involved with Declan, we need—"

"Is that Shar?" she heard Vicky say. "And what do you mean you're not going to let me talk to her? Give me the phone, Blake Michaelsen. Now!"

Shar grinned when she heard the tussling at the other end of the line. And then Winston barked a couple of times in the background, as if in emphasis. Shar loved that dog—and Blake's smart girlfriend.

"Hey, welcome home," Vicky enthused, having apparently won the phone-wrestling match with her brother. "Can't wait to hear all about your California trip."

"Can't wait to tell you about it, Vicky. But...uh, can you go somewhere out of my brother's earshot?"

"Sure." Long pause. "Okay," Vicky whispered. "I'm in the bathroom with the door locked, and Blake was shooting dagger glances at me the whole way. *Mon Dieu*, Shar. What's going on?"

"I need your help. Will you please, *please* keep Blake out of my hair for the weekend? I need to have some breathing room to let a quickie relationship play out, and I need my nosy brother to stay the hell out of it."

"Who is this relationship with?"

"Don't repeat this aloud, okay?"

"Okay."

"Declan Night."

"The hockey player?" she squeaked.

"Vicky!"

"Sorry, sorry. I heard Blake mention Dec's name a few minutes ago, but I never would have guessed—I mean, the guy is super hot, dark, and really knows how to smolder, but he's *so* anti relationships, and—"

"Exactly. It's going to be over in a heartbeat, and that's just what I want."

"Do you, Shar? Do you really?"

"Yes," she insisted, although, perhaps, a tiny little part of her heart protested just a bit. "But if Blake interferes, he'll make everything awkward. Dec and I can begin and end this like adults, but not if my brother gets all protective and starts throwing punches."

Vicky, in her typically French-teacher way, agreed this might be true with a soft *"C'est vrai."* And after another pause, she added, "All right. I'll keep Blake away from you both this weekend...on *one* condition."

"What's that?"

"I want the details," Vicky said, *"All* the sexy details."

CHAPTER FOUR
Saturday At Noon

After Declan dropped Shar off at her condo, he went for a run, ending at Harbor Square so he could pick up his motorcycle. Then he rode home, hopped in the shower, and replayed every delicious second of the night before.

Damn. She was incredible.

He had to switch the water to cool and, then, to icy or he would've stayed in there all day, humping Shar in his mind. He was already looking forward to a replay tonight, more than he should be. Good thing her brother didn't know about any of this or he'd be flattened faster than roadkill.

He wrapped a towel around his waist and wandered into the front room, grinning just thinking about what it was like having Shar here and all the surfaces in his place where he'd kissed her. Touched her.

He checked his cell for messages, and speak of the devil. Voicemail from Blake, left a little less than an hour ago.

"Hey, Dec—funny thing. I was talking to another DJ

from the station, who was at Max's Pub last night. He told me you and my sister were chatting it up at the bar."

Fuck.

Small towns were dangerous places.

The message continued.

"Haven't talked with Shar yet. She's been a little hard to reach this morning. I know I've been kinda preoccupied with Vicky and getting ready for the trip but, uh—give me a call. We should catch up. Soon."

Dec knew that wasn't a *request*, it was fucking demand. He set down his phone. Then he picked it up again, but he didn't dial Blake's number. He called Trevor Cayne in Nashville instead.

"Trev? You got a minute?"

The former *Mirabelle Harbor Gazette* reporter that Dec had known and lived near for years—until the other guy had run off to Tennessee with his redheaded, country-singer girlfriend—said, "Yeah, sure. Shoot."

"Okay. I need to ask you something about Blake."

"If it's about his birthday, you got time, man. It's not until Septem—"

"No. That's not it." Dec took a few deep breaths to try to collect his thoughts. He was usually pretty damn good with words. He was a sportswriter these days, after all, and could explain any play by play in a rink, court, or field like a professional. But though he could use those skills to describe his exploits with women, he didn't want to kiss and tell when it came to Shar. So, he needed to choose his phrases carefully. "Actually, let me ask you something about yourself. When you first met Tina Marie, how did you know she was someone you could be really serious about?"

"There were a few big signs, Dec. I mean, I was crazy attracted to her right away, but that wasn't a new experience. There are a lot of sexy redheads out there." Trev laughed. "What I guess really did it was how comfortable I felt with her *out* of bed, though. The conversations we had in the car or just while walking around. The way it seemed like everything in the universe made sense all of a sudden, just because she was by my side. I can't exactly explain it, but it was like knowing someone would be a good team player on the basketball court. That you could pass to them and could count on them being there to catch the ball. It's instinctive."

Dec hadn't forgotten about Trevor's skill with a basketball. Maybe it wasn't as strong as Dec's slapshot ability with a hockey puck, but it was up there. He had a love of the game—albeit a *different* game—that only other athletes could understand.

"So, what happens when you have a bad throw or she misses the catch?"

"It's not one-hundred percent with anyone," Trev said with a slight chuckle. "But you go into it knowing you've got a good chance at making a decent play most of the time. In the past month since we met, we've had a few misses, but we went into this living arrangement aware we needed to still learn a lot about each other. Openness to that reality has been the key."

"And that's, um...working?"

Trev openly laughed at this. "Yes, Dec."

"Okay. Thanks, man."

"No problem. But what's my relationship with Tina Marie have to do with Blake?"

Dec bit his lip to keep from blurting something stupid like, *Well, I kinda banged his sister, and I'm planning on doing it again. Repeatedly.* He cleared his throat. "I—well, he's getting pretty serious about Vicky, so, I figured talking to you might help me understand this whole long-term relationship thing. Maybe."

"And?"

"And what?"

"And why do you care about understanding it *now?*

Blake's been with Vicky since last fall. Is there a woman in *your* life?"

Dec usually loved his friends, but sometimes he hated the way they were so damned smart. "There, uh, might be someone I kinda connected with."

"Knew it! What's her name and where did you meet her?"

Thankfully, his phone buzzed, indicating another call was coming in and giving him an excuse to hang up on Trev. "She's just someone I met at a bar," he said quickly. "Tell you more about her later, but I gotta grab this call."

"You'd better—" Trev began, but Dec clicked off his phone.

He'd missed the incoming call, but once he realized who'd been calling, he was glad he did.

Blake Michaelsen.

Again.

"I had the strangest conversation with my sister," Blake said in his latest voice message. "I don't have anything to worry about...do I, buddy?"

The term "buddy" was used almost threateningly. Shit. No way could he talk to Blake, not even on the phone, without checking in with Shar first. They needed to corroborate their stories. Plausible deniability only worked if all major parties were in agreement. This he'd learned the hard way in his twenties, after a few near bar brawls, which were the result of him foolishly hitting on the ladylove of some douchebag.

But Sharlene Michaelsen Boyd was no skanky chick. And Blake was one of his best friends.

Not only didn't he want to get Shar in any trouble with her hotheaded bro, but he'd prefer not to get himself punched in the jaw. Dec wasn't as young as he used to be.

He decided to text Blake and tell him the only thing that wasn't completely idiotic, under the circumstances, even if it wasn't entirely honest. "Nope. Nothing to worry about.

Can't talk now, but I'll catch ya later."

A couple minutes later he got a text back. Thankfully, it wasn't from Blake. It was from one of their other friends, Geoff Everest.

"Wanna play some street hockey tonight? One on one at the park—then grab a beer?"

"Can't tonight," he texted back. "Got plans."

"Oooh. With a woman?"

"Maybe," Dec hedged. "Hey, where's your girlfriend?" Geoff and Kelsie were practically inseparable. Dec expected wedding announcements any day now.

"Minneapolis. Some bachelorette party with her college friends," Geoff replied. "Miss her like hell when she's away, but it gives me a chance to hang out with my buds."

"Sorry, man. I can't play this time. Thanks for thinking of me, though."

"Wait—no info on the woman? Dude, you can tell me about her!"

Dec shook his head. No, no, he couldn't. He clicked off without answering Geoff's last text. Let them all think what they wanted. Whatever that was wouldn't be half as incriminating as the truth—he'd slept with one of his best friends' sisters and liked it. A lot. There'd probably be hell to pay, but he'd deal with that later.

After he spent another night with Shar.

Dec was in charge of the food, and he opted for the relative simplicity of Thai, for several reasons:

1. Bangkok Gardens was just down the street from Shar's condo complex, so it had proximity in its favor.

2. They had a pretty healthy selection and featured quite a number of dishes with fresh vegetables, which meant it wouldn't be one of Blake's first five Mirabelle Harbor

dining choices. Probably wouldn't even make the top ten.

3. And, while Dec waited for his order to be ready, he could lightly jog around the block and burn off some of this insane energy. He didn't want to show up at Shar's door looking like he was about to pounce on her. Although, he wanted to. Bad.

He pulled into her lot at 7:02 and waited (almost) patiently for her to let him through the security doors.

His first glimpse of her in eight hours had his heart racing, like in the moments before a big playoff game was set to begin. And, for the next few seconds, he couldn't make his mouth work well enough to speak.

"Hey," she said, her beautiful lips curving into a soft smile.

He wanted her so damn much. But all he could say was "Hey" back.

"So, whatcha got there?" she asked, ushering him inside her place and eyeing the carryout bags.

"Uh." He foisted the Bangkok Gardens bags onto her kitchen counter and began pulling out the various containers and identifying them. Speaking was a little easier when a guy had props. "This one is pad see ewe. This one is sweet and sour pork. There's also beef and broccoli, pan-fried dumplings, and chicken satays. That's dinner."

"Don't you mean that's dinner, our midnight snack, breakfast, *and* lunch tomorrow?"

He grinned. "I wanted you to have options."

"Well done, Declan." She pointed to the smallest bag on the counter, which he hadn't unloaded yet. "What's over there? Monday brunch?"

"Dessert," he replied and pulled out two pints of ice cream—one coconut and one mango.

She put them in the freezer and shot him a gorgeously wicked grin. "We'll have fun with those later."

"God, I hope so." And then he couldn't wait any longer.

He pulled her into his arms and kissed her until they were both panting and breathless. "I'm not really that hungry for anything but you, Shar," he admitted.

"Well, we need to spend at least a few minutes at the table." She waved her palm vaguely in the direction of an oak table set for two. "I left the beverages and accessories there for you to find."

"Accessories?"

He let her lead him to the table, where he saw a sight that actually made his knees go weak—and it had nothing to do with the joint injury he'd gotten in the third period of the second game against Detroit six years ago that'd landed him in physical therapy for two months.

He felt his jaw drop as he took in the bottles of wine, beer, and spirits on the tabletop, which were each decorated with fun little items like padded handcuffs, a blindfold, and...*holy shit*, were those nipple clamps dangling from the rum bottle?

"You stun me, woman," he murmured. "And I'm too damn horny for Thai. Or even alcohol."

She grinned, and her sweet sexiness radiated from her face like sunbeams through the clouds. "I think we should at least have an appetizer or two. To keep our strength up. It's going to be a long and wild night, Dec."

"You promise?"

"Oh, yeah."

"Fine. I'll get the dumplings then," he said. "You can pour us some wine."

She nodded, but the mischievous smile on her face almost unraveled him.

He walked backward toward the kitchen counter, unwilling to tear his gaze away from her. There was something mind-blowing to him about her collection of contradictions. The way she could be both delicate and dangerous simultaneously. Playful and serious. Smokin' hot but also, somehow, so cool and calm and innocent.

It was the mix of tenderness and toughness that got to him most, though. Made him want to both fuck her hard and lightly caress her. To become as contradictory as she was.

"Mmm. Delicious aroma," Shar said, inhaling. They sat down, facing each other. Then she speared a plump dumpling with a wooden chopstick and reached across the table, offering it to him.

He literally had no appetite for any food, no matter how good it might be, but he dutifully took a bite. If Shar was going to feed him, hell, he'd eat.

She eyed the dipping sauce.

He took the chopstick from her hand, dipped the second half of the dumpling in the savory sauce, and reciprocated by bringing it up to her mouth. She pulled it off the stick with her teeth, licked her lips, and chewed.

Was this dinner...or foreplay as a form of torture?

He drank about half his glass of white wine and shook his head.

"What's wrong?" she asked.

"There is not a damn thing that's wrong." Except that time had slowed to a glacial pace, and, if he had to keep looking at those pink satin-lined handcuffs hanging from the neck of the wine bottle, his fantasies would be forever seared with their image.

"Do you like the wine?"

He'd gulped it down without really tasting it, but he nodded. "Do we have to drink the entire bottle before we can use the, um, accessory item attached to it?"

"Nope." Shar swallowed a healthy mouthful of her wine, pushed the container of hot dumplings to the side of the table, and reached for his hand. "Maybe eating and drinking is overrated, huh?"

"It is."

She caressed the length of his fingers—up, down, up— and then abruptly stood, pulling him to his feet along with her. Standing in front of him, she yanked his shirt over his head and ran her palm down his torso, lingering over his abs.

"Impressive," she murmured. "Even more so than last night."

"Why's that?"

"No alcoholic haze impairing my vision, Dec." Then she paused and looked him over so thoroughly, so absorbedly, that he grew even harder under her gaze.

She leaned in, wrapping her lips around his left nipple and sucking. He groaned. She glanced up at him, raising her eyebrows. "No?"

"Yes. That particular sound means *yes*." He nodded for emphasis.

"Good. I want to hear it again." She moved to the right nipple and sucked even harder.

He groaned louder this time. He had no intention of discouraging her.

She laughed, then she unbuckled his belt, dropped his jeans and boxers to the floor, and pushed his naked body toward a wooden, intricately carved, high-back chair with a cushioned leather seat in her living room. No armrests.

"Hands behind your back, behind the chair." She lifted the handcuffs off the wine bottle and dangled them from her index finger.

He grinned. "You like being in charge, don't you?"

"You have no idea."

She snapped the handcuffs on his wrists and retrieved the blindfold from the table. As she firmly covered his eyes with it, he leaned fully back into the seat, waiting.

Every part of him wanted to vibrate at the sexiness of her breath, which he could feel against the top of his head. He could hear her footsteps as she walked around to the front of him, her fingertips trailing a fiery path from his shoulders down to his thighs. She pushed his legs apart with a strength he wouldn't have expected, and he felt her breath there, too, blowing against his straining erection.

Again, he could only wait. Struggle to keep his limbs from shaking from the sheer force of his desire for her.

After an eternity of waiting, he felt the tip of her tongue touch the tip of his cock.

She moved so slowly at first. Circling. Dancing. Teasing.

Then she increased the speed...and the pressure. She took all of him into her mouth. He was bound, blindfolded, and powerless to either see or touch her. Much as he wanted to bury his fingers in those long wavy strands and pull her to him, Dec couldn't do more than surrender to her.

Not that he was complaining.

The heat built up inside him like a boiler on the brink of explosion.

"Shar—"

She did something creative with her tongue and his cock jumped halfway to his chest. *Ohhh, baby!*

"Jesus, Shar. I'm close. Really close. I'm not gonna be able to—"

She took him even deeper, her lips pulsing around him.

It took every ounce of his strength not to burst right then. But just because he loved the way she took charge— had fantasized about being with a woman like this—it didn't mean he didn't have a few ideas of his own.

"I want you to straddle me so I can come inside you," he whispered. "Slide a condom on me and ride me hard. Please, Shar."

She slowly released him and he immediately felt her absence.

"Next time, I'm going to use that fabric as a gag instead of a blindfold," she said, but he could hear the laughter in her voice as she moved away.

But it was just for a few moments. And she did, in fact, do as he asked. In Dec's book, and with a woman as strong-willed as Sharlene Michaelsen Boyd, that counted as more than a tiny triumph.

He heard the distinctive sound of a wrapper being ripped open. Seconds later, the condom was on...and then so was she. The cuffs had completely immobilized his arms, but he imagined embracing her, running his fingers up the creamy skin alongside her spine and getting tangled in her hair.

He couldn't touch her, no. She, on the other hand, let her palms roam freely—sometimes gently, sometimes not.

Dec gasped as he felt a sharp twist and then a metal clamp around his left nipple. He couldn't have been more turned on.

"I thought those were for you, babe," he managed to murmur, gulping in a much-needed lungful of air as she affixed a clamp around his right nipple, too.

"Nope. Not yet anyway. Gentlemen first."

"I'm no gentleman, Shar."

She tugged on the chain that connected the two nipple clamps. The air he'd just inhaled hissed out of his lungs.

"Oh? You will be tonight. Or else." She tugged again, harder. And then she kissed him and rode him and, for what felt like a year and a half, she toyed with him mercilessly. Her hands were the instruments of every kind of sensation—pain, pleasure, surprise, and amazement. Even if he could escape her probing fingers, he wouldn't leave.

"Please take these cuffs off me, so I can touch you."

"Not a chance."

"Then at least release the blindfold."

"Why? Is it too tight? Is it hurting you, Dec?"

He shook his head. "Not at all, but I want to see deep into your eyes. I want to watch your face as you come."

"This again? What is it with you and eye contact?"

"Hey, I want what I want." He dropped his voice to a whisper. "C'mon. Indulge me."

She again tugged on the metal chain, and he would've jumped all the way out of the seat if her slender legs and the weight of her beautiful body hadn't been holding him down.

"Nope. Not this time. Now stop making demands, Dec, and let me kiss you again. I want to feel your tongue tangling with mine when you come. No more damn talking."

So he gave in. He let her have her way with him. Not that he had any choice in the matter, let's face it, but his brain was buzzing with the frenzy of wanting her and he couldn't come up with any reasonable, rational arguments while she was on top of him, sliding in and out and making him lose his fucking mind.

She covered his mouth with hers and, even if he tried, he couldn't argue. Her control of him was complete. A totalitarian takeover of his body and soul.

He came hard and far too quickly after that. Shar writhed on his lap for a few moments more, but he could feel her tightening around him and coming almost as hard.

She didn't move away after her climax. She stayed right there with him, kissing him deeper and bringing them physically even closer than he'd thought possible. Encircling him with all four of her limbs and warming him with the fire of her breath.

Dec longed to touch her back, even more than he wanted to see her, which would've surprised him if he'd been willing to analyze his reactions. But he forced his mind away from that danger zone.

When she finally asked, "What's the first thing you'd like me to remove—the handcuffs, the nipple clamps, or the blindfold?"

Without hesitation, he said, "The cuffs."

She reached behind the chair, flicked the release latch, and let the cuffs drop to the floor.

His arms sprang up around her. And though he could have ditched both the clamps and the blindfold, he didn't bother. All he wanted to do was rub her silky back, knead the muscles in her ass and thighs, cup the fullness of her breasts, and squeeze all the softness and firmness beneath his fingertips. All the sensuality that was Shar.

"I thought *I'd* been in a sexual drought," she teased him. "Don't tell me you haven't gotten laid in months either..."

He unlatched the right nipple clamp from his chest, felt around in the darkness for her nearest nipple, and attached the open end to her. She drew in a quick breath but didn't speak.

"We're similar in more ways than just that," he told her, finally tugging off the blindfold and letting his eyes readjust to the light. God, she was beautiful. He met her gaze and held it. "We're connected on several levels."

"Very clever." She leaned away suddenly and they both flinched from the sharp, unanticipated pain.

He pulled her back to him. "Stay near me," he whispered. "For both our sakes."

She sat very still and in silence for a long time, the seconds ticking by, as he worried that she might be debating the fastest way to end this thing between them tonight. Or, worse, call it a finale on their fling for all nights to come. Hadn't that been exactly what he'd said he wanted just yesterday at the bar? Exactly what she'd said she wanted, too?

Shit.

But after an interminable wait, she didn't announce that it was time to say goodnight. Instead she said, "I didn't expect this, Dec. I didn't expect to...*like* you."

Something in the vicinity of his heart stopped as he tried to wrap his head around what she was telling him. "I didn't expect this either, but sometimes people can't tell what's gonna work until they're, um, together. For, maybe, longer than one night."

"But this is a one-night stand—"

"Technically, it's already been a two-night stand," he

said, grinning at her. "And I'm up for a three-peat tomorrow, if you are."

"You serious?"

He nodded and couldn't help but see the cautiousness in her gaze as she stared at him. "Look, I'm not the most steady date you'll ever have, but even *I* can manage to last a whole weekend. Plus, you know, we've got a couple days worth of Thai food to eat, so we might as well have a few meals together."

That finally made her laugh. "Okay. A three-peat, but then..." She didn't say it, but Dec could almost hear her adding, *But then...we're done.*

Until she let him know that for sure, though, he'd keep it going a bit longer. What harm could come from another night or two (or seven) of mind-blowingly hot sex?

Over cold plates of pad see ewe, beef and broccoli, sweet and sour pork, and chicken satays, Shar asked him, "Why are you still single, Dec? I mean, I'm gun-shy *now*, but I was married once, cheated on, and messily divorced. Was your ex-fiancée so awful that you'd swear off a committed relationship forever?"

He shrugged. "She used me, Shar." Shitty memories had him shuddering internally, but he tried not to show it. "Trish didn't care about me, just my 'status.' She was the poster girl for the perfect team groupie, and she played the role better than most. Fooled me into believing it was more than it was. But when I left professional hockey, she lost interest in me. Fast."

"Stupid, superficial chick," he heard Shar mutter. "I hadn't realized. Sorry, Dec. You're just so much like Blake, and the two of you have been buddies for so many years that I sometimes forget that you're a much bigger celebrity."

He cocked an eyebrow at her. "Let's get this one thing straight, babe—in the most important of ways, I am *nothing* like your brother."

She laughed and pointedly peeked under the table at his crotch and his hastily donned boxers, which were sporting a growing erection. Nothing "brotherly" about that, no. And there was no mistaking how much he wanted her—again. This time, though, he'd be the one in control. Maybe. If she let him.

The thought made him smile. He reached over to hand-feed her a juicy pineapple chunk from the sweet and sour pork and she pulled it directly from his fingers and licked her lips.

He raised his eyebrows in invitation. She raised hers back. And then—

The phone rang. Her landline.

She ignored it. Whoever called didn't leave a message.

But then her cell rang.

And while she was checking that—"Julia," she said. "I'll call her back later"—he checked his own phone. A series of texts from Geoff asking how things were going with the "mystery woman."

Then, literally, less than a minute later, her cell phone beeped with an incoming message—"Vicky this time," she explained, turning slightly pink as she read it—and his rang with a call from Trev. He let it go to voicemail. But, then, he listened to the message.

"What the fuck is going on up there?" his friend in Nashville said. "Blake just called me. With *questions*."

Dec forced a laugh when Shar eyed him curiously from across the room.

"Well, shit," he said. "We're popular tonight, huh?"

"Yeah."

"Do you, um, wanna answer calls from our friends or...do something else?"

She tossed her cell back on the counter, but she didn't walk toward him. She headed to the refrigerator instead. He squinted at her. They'd eaten a mountain of Thai food. Was she still hungry?

"I want to do something with this." She pulled open the freezer door and retrieved the pint of mango ice cream.

Ah. Now that was more like it.

He set down his phone and pointed toward the silverware drawer. "Spoons or no spoons?"

"I'll let you decide *that*." She sauntered toward her bedroom. "But I'll be waiting in here. You coming?"

Hell, yeah.

CHAPTER FIVE
Sunday Morning

Shar couldn't bring herself to break off this fling too quickly. She'd agreed to Dec's suggestion of a three-peat last night because it felt more like a weekend-long one-night stand, rather than three separate dates, even if it was technically the latter.

And, well, she wasn't an idiot.

Why refuse a Sunday-night "hat trick," as Dec, always the hockey player, had so humorously called it this morning, when the sex between them had been phenomenal for the first two nights?

Tomorrow, though, it would be all over. Back to her regularly scheduled singleton status.

She exhaled as they got ready to part, weirdly aware that this thought didn't bring her much pleasure. She was usually so damn relieved when an inappropriate fling was winding down. Maybe it was because Declan Night was someone she might run into again fairly soon. Or because he had ties to her brother. Or even because he'd been a surprisingly fun conversationalist over the past few days.

Not to mention, sexy as hell.

It's just the loneliness talking, she told herself. *It'll pass.*

Dec had a story to write today, something sports related for the *Mirabelle Harbor Gazette*, and he said he needed to check in on his store. "I've only got a few employees," he told her. "But they're great guys. I know The Penalty Box is in good hands when I'm not there, but I don't like to take them for granted."

Shar could appreciate this. And she had work to do, too. She'd been putting off moving a few boxes of school supplies into her classroom and organizing several sets of novels that came in for her eighth graders while she was out in L.A. Some Jane Austen, some Harper Lee, some Will Shakespeare—the usual classics, and for good reason. She'd also promised Julia that she'd check in on her house.

"How 'bout you meet me at my place tonight, around six?" Dec suggested.

"Sure." She thought about her day. "It's possible I'll be finished a bit earlier—"

"Even better. Let's make it five then. Okay?"

As she readily agreed, she found herself—*again!*—perplexed by her own reactions. Why was she so anxious to see him tonight when he hadn't even left her condo yet this morning? It wasn't as though they hadn't already spent a shocking number of hours in each other's company this weekend. She should be sick of him by now—*and vice versa!*—not practically counting the minutes until they could be together again.

Then he kissed her goodbye...and she could no longer remember what her arguments were about meeting early or seeing him for three nights in a row. A hat trick, indeed.

Once Shar managed to pull herself together, she grabbed her car keys and drove over to Julia's house. She walked around the property, watered the plants, made sure there were no issues Julia needed to know about, and then she gave her BFF a quick call.

"Hey, girlfriend. Just wanted to let you know that your white rose bushes are blooming and that you have a few cherry tomatoes on the—"

"Seriously, Shar? You're giving me a vegetation update?"

"Well, yeah. I thought you'd want to know—"

"The *only* thing I want to know is what's happening with you and Declan." Julia huffed in exasperation and Shar could almost see her rolling her eyes. "I've aged half a millennium just waiting for you to answer my text from last night! Details. *Now!*"

Shar laughed. "When did you become so pushy? I'm not kidding. You're starting to sound as impatient as me. Is it, like, a California thing? I thought they were all so laidback out there."

"When I fly home, the first thing I'm going to do is show up at your place and strangle you. Now...spill."

Much as Shar enjoyed teasing her best friend, the situation with Dec was actually too bizarre for her to keep entirely to herself. She'd never needed a large number of confidantes—and, hell, with four brothers and no sisters, it wasn't like she had a lot of family options growing up—but she'd always relied on a handful of trusted friends to talk through the most perplexing situations in her life. And nothing had confused her more in recent years than these past few days with Declan.

"I don't understand my responses to him. I'm not talking physically," she admitted to Julia. "I get that part. And it's *good*. But I mean emotionally. Nothing about this fling of ours is normal for me. It was supposed to be over already. We both agreed. And yet..."

"What?"

"He and I have plans together. Again. Tonight."

Julia mumbled something.

"Say what?"

"Maybe it's not a fling, Shar."

"Of course it is! I told you it was. Dec and I agreed it was. It *has* to be."

Her friend cleared her throat. "I know you probably don't want to hear this, but just because two people agree on something, it doesn't mean that's what's actually going to happen. Two people can, for instance, take a vow in front of a preacher saying they'll love, honor, and be faithful to each other until death, and that might not always be how it goes down."

Julia's voice was gentle but very serious. Shar swallowed. She hardly needed a reminder of Stephen's infidelity. The asshat. But she acknowledged what her friend was telling her.

"Likewise," Julia continued, "two people can claim they're just friends or that their relationship isn't 'real' or whatever, and that could be a lie, too. Or, you know, a staggering and inconceivable understatement."

This, too, Shar understood very well, especially from her friend's point of view. For the longest time, Julia, who'd become a widow way too young, hadn't believed she and her movie-star boyfriend could have a real relationship. They almost lost each other as a result of that. And, given the whole Hollywood-actor, teen-idol thing, the progression of their love story *had* been pretty unusual and unexpected. But no one who knew Julia and Dane could doubt they belonged together.

"So, when I suggest that, perhaps, what you and Declan are experiencing might not be what you'd anticipated," Julia concluded, "I'm not making judgments or questioning your intentions. You're one of the smartest and most honest people I know. I'm just stating *one* possibility that I don't think you should be so quick to overlook."

Shar felt tears prick the corners of her eyes. An odd, unwelcome sensation that she always tried hard to fight. She wanted to be so tough. So unflappable. So resilient that nothing and no one could hurt her ever again.

But if Julia was right—and if she allowed herself to open her heart to someone like Declan Night, even for just a short but genuine relationship—she knew she could get crushed. That was the very real consequence of having a *relationship*, not merely a fling. And she couldn't put herself in the line of fire that way. Especially not with a man who was just as committed to remaining unattached as she was.

"Thanks, girlfriend," she whispered. "I hear you. I do. It's just...I don't think someone like me entertaining thoughts like these about somebody like him is a good idea. For either of us."

"What do you mean by 'someone like you,' Shar? Someone intelligent, talented, generous, and loyal? Just because that bastard ex-husband of yours didn't know how to recognize a wonderful woman when he had her in front of him, it doesn't mean another man would be as foolhardy. Especially not somebody as clever as Dec. My boyfriend did some research on him, you know."

Okay. Shar was listening. "Really?"

"Oh, yeah."

"And what did the formidable Dane Tyler, aka, Guru of the Google Search, discover, hmm?"

"He said—" There was a squeal on the other end of the line, and Shar could hear Julia calling out, "Give me my phone back! I'm talking to my best friend. You can't just snatch—"

There was a pause and some scuffling noises, followed by something that sounded suspiciously like kissing.

"Hey, you annoying lovebirds," Shar said, feigning irritation. "I'm not gonna listen to an X-rated scene on my phone. I'll be hanging up now—"

"No wait, Shar," a deep male voice that had melted the hearts of millions of moviegoers around the world said to her. "As Julia told you, I looked up your man, and—"

"He's not my man."

"Whatever you say, ma'am," Dane replied, adopting a smooth Southern gentleman accent this time. "I'm just-a lettin' you know that Declan Night is a mighty fine gent, at least I reckon that's so." He returned to his normal voice. "He's no dumb jock, that's for sure. Not only did he get a full-ride college scholarship to Princeton, but he graduated with a business degree in three and a half years, before he was drafted to the NHL. More impressively, he was never at the center of any sports scandal. He never punched out any reporters. And he never even sounded like an A-hole during any of his TV interviews. Probably why he wasn't as well known as several of his less articulate teammates."

It hadn't occurred to her to watch YouTube clips of Dec giving interviews, but that was only because he'd seemed to have put his hockey-player past behind him. He appeared content to be a sportswriter and a business owner now. Seemed to want nothing to do with the fame and special perks bestowed on professional athletes.

There'd been talk in Mirabelle Harbor a few years back about why he'd retired fairly young, but based on what Dec had shared with her about his ex-fiancée, Trish, Shar didn't blame him from stepping away from the spotlight.

"That was probably by design," she said to Dane. "He isn't the type to seek out unnecessary attention."

"My point exactly," he replied. "He's a clever man, who knows the score when it comes to that celebrity shit. And the fact that he likes you and wants to spend more time with you only confirms his intelligence."

She blushed. She wasn't any less immune to the charms of Dane Tyler than most women, but she'd also just spent a couple of weeks at his L.A. home, and she knew that, while Dane had a good heart, he wasn't prone to false flattery. In private and with those he trusted, he dropped his guard like a curtain falling.

"It means a lot to me that you think so, Dane, but—"

"But nothing, Shar. Listen to me on this, okay? A man can look good on paper but be bad in person. The reverse is also true. God knows, I've seen enough examples of both. But no matter what he might say—or what others might say *about* him—his actions will speak the truth. Just watch him. Watch what he does. If there's a discrepancy between his words and his behavior, you'll know which one to believe."

As Shar was in the middle of unpacking the novels in her classroom that afternoon, her cell phone went crazy. Like eight texts in as many seconds.

Vicky.

"I've been patient," her first text read.

"What's going on with Dec?"

"Are you with him now?"

"You *promised* me details if I'd keep your brother off your back."

"I don't take promises lightly, Shar."

"Also, I'm not above blackmail."

"Text me or call me or I'll start dropping hints to Blake," Vicky threatened. This rant was followed by another text filled with a string of evil-grin emojis.

Great.

She immediately texted her sweet but prying friend.

"I thought you were a good Catholic girl from Indiana," she typed. "Blackmailing one's friends is immoral, or did you forget that?"

Vicky's reply was nearly instantaneous. "I haven't been a good Catholic in a long time. And I've been living in sin with your brother for most of this year...or did you forget that?"

Shar laughed. Blake and his girlfriend were thick as

thieves—if those thieves were only stealing time away from the world so they could screw like teenagers. "How could I?" she replied. "Blake's never been happier."

And, mystifying as it was to see her formerly commitment-adverse brother so smitten, it was also the God's honest truth. Shar wasn't one to get all gushy via text message, but she was pretty sure Vicky had saved Blake's life last year. Literally. She'd pulled him back from the brink of self destruction, for sure. Much as Shar had been avoiding a serious relationship herself, she'd always be grateful her brother had found Vicky when he did.

"Aww..." Vicky wrote. "That's so sweet. Now enough procrastination. What's going on with you & Hockey Dude?"

Shar managed to give her an abbreviated, although (mostly) truthful, account of the last few days. "There's no bullshit with Dec," she added. "For either of us, really. He already knows I'm messed up, and he is, too."

"Sounds like a catch," Vicky wrote. "LOL."

Shar laughed. "That's why it should be a short-term thing."

"Wow. But still... You and I need to get together next week before Blake and I leave to Paris."

"You probably have a lot to do."

"For you? I'll make time, Shar."

Shar wasn't entirely sure if this was more a promise or a threat.

"And I'm excited for you," Vicky added.

"It's *way* too early for excitement. And please, please keep any speculation away from my brother, okay? Dec and I might not even be on 'occasionally texting' terms by the time you two get back from your trip."

"Fine. I'll play along and keep all this on the down low," the insatiably romantic French teacher wrote. "But I think you should know something about *l'amour*...or even *l'engouement*."

"Say what?"

"Love or infatuation, Shar. The chance to really connect with someone is a gift. Whether it's for a few days or for a lifetime, it's worth it. If it's real."

Someone else lecturing her about what was real and true and blah, blah, blah. She wasn't about to argue, but she had the sneaking suspicion that just about everyone in her life was conspiring to tell her that they knew better than she did about what her heart needed.

It was getting pretty damn irritating.

To complete the triumvirate of well-meaning female friends, who were sure they had the answers to every freakin' thing about relationships, was her beautiful, loving, and oh-so-inquisitive sister-in-law, Olivia Michaelsen. Married to Shar's eldest brother, Derek, for nearly thirteen years now, Shar and Olivia had bonded like true sisters from the jump. They stopped by each other's places unannounced. Finished each other's sentences half the time. Never shied away from asking blunt questions.

Shar had never considered this unusual, annoying, potentially problematic, or even remotely intrusive.

Until today.

"I stopped by your condo," Olivia said, crossing her arms and leaning against the doorframe of her classroom. "You weren't there."

Shar nodded noncommittally. "That's 'cause I was here."

"Were you also here yesterday morning?"

"Yesterday...?"

Her sister-in-law arched both of her thin blond brows. "I stopped by then, too. Saturday morning. With fruit."

Shar felt her jaw drop. "Oh, no! The farmer's market."

The two of them had made tentative plans to go to it together. Downtown Mirabelle Harbor was a splendor of sights and scents on Saturday mornings in summer. But the best pickings were first thing in the morning, of course, and she'd completely forgotten about it. Because she'd been in bed. With Declan. At his place. And even hearing her sister-in-law's cheery voice message hadn't jogged her memory yesterday. "I'm so sorry, Olivia."

The other woman shrugged good-naturedly. "I figured you might've forgotten because of the jetlag and all. You've only been home from California for a few days."

Shar nodded, but that wasn't even close to the real reason.

From the look on Olivia's face, her brother's wife wasn't entirely buying it either. Especially when she added, "But I couldn't figure out why you didn't hear me knocking on your door at eight a.m. Or why you didn't pick up your landline when I called. Or even your cell."

Shar stared at her helplessly. Her family and friends had left a gazillion messages during the course of the weekend but, of course, she'd been otherwise occupied.

"There must've been one heck of a weird disturbance in the force here in Mirabelle Harbor these past few days," Olivia continued. "With Derek gone for hours at a time, Blake all hyped up and asking questions about you, Chance being especially secretive, and even Nia being a little cagey." She paused and wandered into the classroom, closer to Shar. "Although, fortunately, I finally figured out what was going on with your kid brother and his girlfriend and, also, why my hubby seemed to never be home in the past two days."

A bolt of worry shot through her, and Shar caught her breath. "Everything okay?"

Her sister-in-law took a few more steps toward her, until they were less than a yard apart. "They're all fine, and it's really good news, so you're lucky. The family's got enough of a distraction to keep most of them from piecing together whatever it is you've been hiding."

Shar grimaced at Olivia's smug expression, but she only said, "Good news?"

"Yep. Guess who just popped the question?"

It took Shar a few nanoseconds before the thrilling realization washed over her. "Oh, my goodness! Chance and Nia?"

Olivia nodded.

Shar squealed, and the two of them immediately began clapping their hands and jumping up and down in the middle of her junior high classroom.

"When did it happen?" she asked when they finally stopped to catch their breath.

"About an hour ago. Derek has been assisting Nia all weekend in her preparations."

"Wait—what?"

"Apparently, Chance had already asked Nia to marry him. Like a month or something after they'd met," Olivia explained. "She wasn't ready then, but he insisted that he'd wait for her. And she's ready now. So, she asked your big brother to keep Chance occupied so she could set up the big surprise. And then Derek and Nia got all of Chance's coworkers at Harbor Fitness in on it. Turned the sauna at the gym into a tropical paradise."

"The sauna?" Shar repeated. "Kind of an odd place to propose, but I guess it could come close to tropical temperatures, right?"

Olivia laughed. "Yeah. Nia refused to elaborate on her choice of location, but Chance must have liked it. He apparently said yes within seconds. Not that we could get him to spill any other details..." She shook her head. "The two of them are just so darned cute."

"They are," Shar agreed.

"Oh, and we're going to host a Michaelsen family engagement party for them at our house this Friday, before

Blake and Vicky take off to France."

"I'll be there! And I'll help." She clapped her hands again. This was going to be *fun*. A happy Michaelsen occasion to look forward to—finally. They'd had too many funerals in the past. "Do we know when the wedding will be?"

"It's looking like Christmastime." Then, after a beat. "Hey, do you already have a Plus One in mind?" Olivia swiveled on her sneaker soles and sashayed back toward the door, then she shot a knowing glance over her shoulder.

Shar tried to school her face into an expression of neutrality and guilelessness. "Uh..."

Her sister-in-law smirked. "'Cuz I'm betting you do."

CHAPTER SIX

Sunday Afternoon

The first thing Declan did after he left Shar's condo was to go straight to the Mirabelle Harbor High School track and run a sub six-minute mile. He had to clear his head.

When sprinting didn't do the trick, he went back to his place and played "Puck You," his favorite hockey video game, for over an hour. Better, but still not nearly enough.

Geoff had texted last night, and that was easier to respond to than Trevor's voice message. So he sent a standard—if somewhat fictitious—reply to the former:

"Doing fine! How are things going for you? Kelsie back from Minnesota yet?"

Geoff's text back came swiftly. "First, you're lying. Second, you clearly weren't paying enough attention before. Kelsie's gone ALL weekend. Which, under normal circumstances would mean you and I would be hanging out. The fact that we're *not* means something major is going on. See point number one—you're lying."

"Okay, I'm NOT fine. Satisfied?"

"Of course not. Need company, Dec?"

"Thanks, but no. Not today. Have to finish this story for the paper. But I may need you to help me rally my spirits if the 'something major' I have going on turns south."

"I'm here for you," his photographer buddy wrote. "You know that."

He did. And, fortunately, his friend let him off the hook. For now, at least.

So as not to fully deserve Geoff's accusation of being a liar, Dec actually did work on the revisions for the *Gazette* sports feature he'd promised his boss, Lillian. He emailed it to her and then shut down his laptop.

Now what?

He forced himself to listen to Blake's and Trevor's various messages (there were several), and decided to bite the bullet and call his buddy in Nashville.

"Hey, Trev. I didn't wake you, did I?"

"Hardly. It's one thirty in the afternoon. You a little hung over today, Dec?"

Was he?

Nope. Not a bit.

This crazy, unsettled feeling of being vaguely ill was not alcohol induced. He knew the difference. This was Shar.

"No," he said. He could hear a beautiful voice singing in the background. "Wow. Is that Tina Marie?"

"Yeah, she's amazing." The pride in his friend's voice couldn't be disguised. "She's writing a new song, and I love hearing her work. The artistry and magical synthesis when it all comes together is incredible."

"It's very cool," he agreed.

"Definitely. And we could talk about creativity and the creative process all day if, in fact, we'd *ever* had a conversation about something like that in our *entire* friendship or, you know, if that was remotely on your mind. Now, cut the crap, Dec, and tell me what the hell is going on up there. Blake's called here a bunch of times, grilling me about whether I'd heard from you and if I 'knew anything' that he should know about."

Dec held his breath for a moment and exhaled slowly before speaking. "What'd you say?"

"I said I didn't know shit about what was going on with you because that's *almost* true. I know you mentioned that you'd connected with someone you'd met in a bar, but you damn well neglected to mention that it was *Sharlene*." The pause on the line was interminable. "You must be out of your fucking mind to be shagging Blake's sister."

"*Shagging?* What are you British all of a sudden? Just because you're writing for an international magazine these days..." Trevor had left the *Gazette* when he moved to Tennessee and now wrote for several publications, both foreign and domestic.

"I happen to prefer that term to humping or screwing or other variants, so sue me. But the statement still stands, Dec. You must be out of your—"

"I'm crazy about her," he blurted. "I know it's probably gonna cause a rift between Blake and me, and that sucks, it really does. But I can deal with it if Shar's willing to. I just—I just—"

"What? What is it about her that makes you feel this crazy way?"

Dec knew his buddy was sincerely asking, but he also suspected Trev was trying to gently lead him to a reasonable explanation. And Dec didn't have one. He just liked being with Shar. And he liked himself more when they were together. "There's no front with her, you know? She's not faking anything with me. I don't feel like I have to try to impress her or that she expects me to perform a role for her."

"Because she knows you and is already wowed by you?"

He laughed. "Nope. Because she knows me and *knows better* than to be wowed. She doesn't give a shit about my hockey past. I'm not sure she could even differentiate between a goalie's stick and a right winger's, but together we never seem to run out of things to say."

"Does she have any idea you're thinking about her this way? This seriously?"

"God, no. It's just the opposite," he admitted miserably. "She's convinced this is, at most, a weekend fling. That it'll all disappear tomorrow morning. That we don't even have to *tell* Blake about it because it's almost over and we'd just get him all riled up for nothing."

"Dec, if Blake doesn't already know for sure about the two of you, he *strongly* suspects."

"Yeah, no shit. What is it with that family? Everyone knows—or thinks they know—everything about everybody all the fucking time."

Trevor laughed. "My Gram Bernadette and Tina Marie's folks are like that. Love 'em all but, honestly, it's safer to be a few states away sometimes."

Dec pondered this after he clicked off his cell. Could he whisk Shar away to somewhere else, like Colorado or D.C.? Or maybe further—London, Australia, or Istanbul? Not that he wanted to leave Mirabelle Harbor, but that might give them a shot at an authentic, open, unobstructed-by-her-brother romance.

Then again, Blake wasn't one to let a few (thousand) air miles stop him. Dec would probably lose a few teeth before this was all over, whether or not Shar was even willing to give an actual relationship with him a try.

And the fact that Dec was even *thinking* thoughts like these meant he'd officially become a lunatic. Falling for a woman? Being willing to move somewhere just to be with her? Wanting a real relationship?

Yeah. He'd lost his effing mind...right along with his heart.

It was nearly five p.m. when Shar arrived at The Penalty Box. Early by ten minutes, but she couldn't wait to see Declan again. Less than forty-eight hours with the guy and she'd been reduced to acting like a teenage girl before prom. What the heck was wrong with her?

Still, she pushed the door open and meandered inside. Dec and only two other people—one college-aged employee and one elderly gentleman customer—were left in the store, probably since it was so close to closing time.

Dec saw her at once, smiled at her so radiantly that her heartbeat quickened, and waved her over to the back. "Glad you're here," he said. "I'm just letting Marcus finish helping his customer, but then we can lock up and go upstairs. I've got a few dinner ideas."

She lowered her voice and asked, "To eat or to play games with?"

He grinned. "Both."

The college kid—Marcus—dressed in a Blackhawks hockey jersey that passed for a "uniform" in Dec's fine sportswear establishment, thanked his customer as he left, said a polite hello to Shar, and then told Dec he'd take care of adding up the day's receipts.

"Nah," Dec replied. "I can handle it. It's nice outside. Why don't you knock off early and catch a few rays while you can. I'll see you tomorrow."

"You sure?" Marcus said.

"Yep." Dec motioned for him to go, and the kid didn't waste any time. He grabbed his backpack and, with a friendly salute, took off.

Dec glanced at the clock. Five minutes to five. "I'm not expecting anyone else to show up this late. Just let me cash out the register and we can head upstairs, okay?"

"Okay." Her pulse seemed intent on drag racing

through her body. She liked being with him so, so much. Tomorrow morning, when their wild weekend was over, she knew she'd feel the loss of his company...but there was still tonight, and she planned to enjoy it.

Then he kissed her, and *oh, boy.*

It was different this time. She couldn't deny that. Passionate, yes, but also, somehow, familiar, like it was the most natural thing in the world that they could do. Not merely a weekend novelty, but the act of a normal, everyday couple.

One of the few things she'd liked about her first and only marriage was that she and Stephen had achieved that level of familiarity and intimacy. She'd never expected to feel it with someone else after that. And she especially hadn't expected to feel it with someone she'd been "dating," for want of a better word, for so short a time.

Her lips were still tingling from his kiss when she heard bells. Wow. He *was* good.

Then she realized the bells were attached to the front door, which jingled when a last-minute customer had entered the shop.

Dec pulled his gaze away from her to greet the new person. "Hey, we're about to close, but if you need something partic—" His words stopped, and every muscle in his face froze.

Shar glanced across the room at the door. It took her longer than it should have to identify the customer. Or, rather, her brother.

"Blake?" she whispered.

Her unsmiling sibling took several strides toward them as she and Dec stood side by side and motionless by the cash register. Dec's arm suddenly tightened around her shoulder protectively and, again, her heartbeat sped up. He wasn't running away at the first sight of a formidable opponent. A brave—though probably foolish—man.

When Blake got about four or five feet away from

them, he leaned against a shelf packed with various hockey team T-shirts, crossed his arms, and said, "I just had to see this for myself."

"See, um, what?" Shar asked, staring hard at him.

Blake raised both of his dark eyebrows and pierced her with a look. "Seriously? That's how you're gonna play it, Sis?" Then the brows dropped and he leveled a threatening glare at his good friend. "One of my best buddies...with my only sister. As I recall, Dec, I warned you about this *years* ago."

"Blake, now listen," Dec said in a surprisingly calm and even tone. "For all those years, I didn't touch her. Not even once. I barely even let myself look at her. But things changed Friday night." He paused and took a long breath. "If Shar tells me to leave her the hell alone, I will. Right now and for all time. But *no one* else gets to say so. Not even *you*."

Then Dec turned to look at her, his eyes asking questions she'd never expected to have to answer. She wasn't sure what words to say aloud, but if Dec thought she'd bail on him tonight, just because Blake was trying to intimidate them both, he didn't know her *nearly* well enough.

She smiled at him, stepped closer, and squeezed. His arm tightened even more around her.

"Is that so?" her brother asked, taking several strides forward.

"It is," Dec replied, not budging from his spot. "Shar, would you like to go upstairs with me and spend the evening together as we originally planned?"

She found her voice. "I sure would, Dec."

Blake rolled his eyes like a spoiled toddler. "You realize he's a commitment-phobe, right, Sis?"

Shar laughed. "Blake, *I'm* a commitment-phobe, or have you missed the truckload of memos I've sent our family since my divorce? Declan is no worse than me.

75

Now, buzz off and go study your French. You need the practice. And here's a phrase to get you started: *Occupe-toi de tes oignons*. Or, just in case you don't know that one, 'Mind your own business.' Got it?"

Blake didn't speak for the longest time, but his face got increasingly redder, and it looked as though he would soon explode. He was actually shaking... It took her several moments to figure out that it wasn't from rising fury.

It was laughter. So much laughter that he was rocking in place from the sheer force of trying to contain it.

And then he burst.

Dec squinted at him. Then he looked at her.

Shar shrugged. "I have no idea what he's been snorting this afternoon, but I may have to call Vicky and give her a heads up."

Blake waved his hands, still doubled over and laughing like a jester in some Elizabethan comedy. She kinda wanted to smack him.

"No, no," her brother said. "She'd say I was interfering, but I really just had to see this with my own eyes. You two are fucking *perfect* for each other. I've thought so for, like, half a decade, but I was too afraid you'd kill each other if you hooked up too soon."

"What?" Dec said, his jaw dropping.

"WHAT?" Shar said, stunned and more than a little pissed. She could've been with Dec right after her first marriage imploded. She could've saved herself the calamity of those awful post-divorce dating experiences. She could've had mind-altering sex with him *years* ago...well, maybe not. She might not have appreciated the kind of man he was back then. And, maybe, he wouldn't have been as receptive to her either.

She and Dec exchanged a glance and then stared at her brother.

"He's one of my best friends, Shar," Blake explained. "I love him like a brother, but he was no good for a woman like you five or six years ago. I know he's been burned since then, and that made him cautious and more sensitive. You're strong-willed, sassy, and very smart. Please go easy on him, okay?"

Shar nodded mutely at him.

"Good," Blake said. Then to his buddy, "And she's my little sister, Dec. I'll beat you to a fucking pulp if you hurt her or betray her like that douchebag ex of hers. You know I'll do it."

"He *will* do it," Shar murmured.

"Yeah, I'm aware," Dec said.

"Fine. Now that we're all clear, I need to get back home because my girlfriend has been texting me nonstop and warning me not to bother you two little lovebirds—*or else*." He laughed. "She's so adorable. But I don't wanna make her mad." He took a few steps toward the door. "Oh, just some advice. You might want to lock this front door if you, you know, got any really kinky stuff planned—"

Dec picked up a loose hockey puck from a bucket on the counter and pitched it at Blake. Hard. Her brother ducked just in time and scooted closer to the exit.

Blake held up his palm. "Now hold on, just one more thing. Chance and Nia's engagement party. This coming Friday night. Michaelsen manor. Six o'clock. Be there."

"I already know about it," Shar said, her fingers itching to throw a puck at her brother as well. "Olivia told me this afternoon."

"I'm not talking to *you*. I'm talking to *him*." He nodded at Declan. "It's a family thing, but you know you're invited now, right?"

Shar groaned and turned toward the man whose arm was still wrapped around her. "Oh, God, Dec. You don't have to go to this. You're going to be *so* harassed by my pain-in-the-ass brothers and—"

"I don't doubt it," he said with a steely, challenging look at Blake. "But you're worth it, Shar."

She didn't know exactly what happened next or why, but it was as if his sweet and sincere words unraveled something tight and knotted deep in her soul. The unexpected release brought tears to her eyes, and she bit her lip to try to keep the emotion from flowing. Gratitude and affection, that was what it was. And she felt it for him. So powerfully, it almost undid her.

"Good answer, Dec," Blake said softly. Then with a wink—*a flipping wink!*—he slipped outside and disappeared.

"You okay?" Dec asked her, seeing her tears and looking worried.

She nodded and smiled at him, hoping he could read the incredible fondness she felt for him. "I'm just...I'm falling for you, Dec."

He pulled her to him so fast, and clung to her so hard, that she would have had to fight him with all her strength if she'd wanted to break free.

But, oh, she didn't.

She wanted to stay in his warm embrace for...well, who knew how long? But it was going to be for more than today, if she got her wish.

"C'mon," he whispered. "Let's go up to my place."

He closed the cash register, bolted shut the shop door, and took her hand.

When they were safely upstairs in his apartment, he turned her to face him and put both of her hands on his heart.

"Shar, I'm a lousy boyfriend. I have the suckiest track record imaginable for long-term relationships. But I'm as crazy about you as I am the NHL playoffs, the light on Lake Michigan at dawn, and mango ice cream in bed."

She almost giggled. They'd had some serious fruit-flavored fun last night. And they still hadn't cracked open that pint of creamy coconut yet.

"Dec, I distrust men. I like having my own space and

following my own schedule. But ever since we started talking on Friday at Max's, I've been hoping for the oddest things—like that our one-night stand might turn into a one-week or a one-month stand—or even longer. It scares me to want anything that smacks of true commitment, but I can't deny what I feel for you."

He nodded. "I get that. All of the parts of that. We don't need to make future plans, though, to keep moving forward. Every single day—and every night—with you would be a gift, in my opinion. More than I ever expected to get. So, I'm gonna cherish our moments together, no matter how long they last."

"Me, too," she agreed. "And now it's day or, uh, night...number three."

"But who's counting?"

She grinned. "We both are, and you know it."

He laughed. "True."

"That doesn't mean we've got to limit it, though," she told him. "Let's see if we can last so long that we get into double or even triple digits. What do you say?"

"I say that sounds like a worthy goal. And, maybe," he added, "if we get really lucky, we'll finally lose count."

Much later that night, lying in bed with the radio on, they were enjoying a long string of purely romantic hits. Music Shar and Dec had to admit they hadn't been able to listen to without a pang of sadness and regret for far too long.

They'd tuned into 102.5 "LOVE" FM, Mirabelle Harbor's only radio station and the one where Blake was one of the regular DJs.

DJ Amelia Lockett signed off with a pair of swoony favorites—"I'll Make Love to You" by Boyz II Men and

Thomas Rhett's "Die a Happy Man."

Then it was time for Blake's shift, which he started with the Foo Fighters and their hit "Everlong."

They were lying face to face, and Dec trailed his fingers up her side, from her hip to her neck, caressing gently. Then, not so gently, he rolled her on top of him and said, "Have your way with me, woman. I'm yours."

"Again?" Shar laughed. She couldn't get enough of him, though. "Okay, but turn off that radio. I don't think I can listen to my brother saying *anything* without it distracting me, no matter how sexy you are."

"Done," he said, reaching for the stereo's remote. But before he could flick it off, Blake's voice came on the air.

"This next tune goes out to a pair of couples that I care about deeply, as they both celebrate taking a leap of faith and some first steps in a new direction. Chance and Nia...Sharlene and Declan...this is for all four of you." And then Blake played a song that made her smile.

Etta James. "At Last."

Dec met her gaze and held it for a long, long time, as they both listened to the lyrics. "Yeah," he whispered after a minute. "That's it exactly. Just as she sang."

"Yeah," Shar agreed before she leaned down to kiss him. Life *was* like a song.

A beautiful one.

BONUS: ABBY COMES HOME

~A preview from *Rocket Man*, a Mirabelle Harbor novella, coming soon!~

Sunday, Late October

Abby Solinski's flight from Sarasota to Chicago touched down four minutes ahead of schedule and taxied smoothly toward the Arrivals gate. Not that it mattered. Her brother, Allan, was picking her up from O'Hare, and he'd never been on time—let alone early—for anything in his entire, charmingly irresponsible life.

She had a full half hour to meander down to the baggage claim carousels, retrieve her luggage, text her best friends in Florida to let them know she'd landed safely, and eat the second half of a PB&J sandwich she'd packed for the trip...all before she spotted her big brother's dark red truck angling for a space in the pick-up lane.

"Hey, Sis!" Allan called out with a wave through his open window.

"Hey, yourself," she called back and motioned for him

to stay inside the vehicle. She had no trouble hefting her bags into the bed of the truck by herself, and she figured the sooner they got on the road, the better.

"Are we going home first or directly to the rehab center?" she asked, slipping into the passenger seat and fastening her seatbelt. Allan had a lead foot.

Her brother grinned at her. "Nice to see you, too, Abby. Missed you."

She laughed. Always late, but always a sweetheart. At least deep down. That was her brother. "Missed you, too. But you know, Mom and Dad have me worried. What's the status today?"

He wrinkled his nose and glanced at the clock on the dashboard. "Dad's rehab session will be over for the afternoon by the time we get to Mirabelle Harbor, so we'd do better to head straight to the house. The doc said he's had a pretty bad knee and ankle injury, especially given his age, but he's hobbling around well enough, all things considered. It's Mom that's the bigger problem."

Allan didn't have to spell out the issues. She knew this story—every chapter, every verse, every predictable ending—because she'd lived it. And so had Allan. Their mom was a *hoverer* of the highest order. When one of her loved ones was sick, injured, or in any way indisposed, Jackie Solinski wouldn't leave that person's side. It was simultaneously endearing and suffocating.

"Has Dad announced that he's running away yet?"

Her brother laughed. "Only three times this weekend."

It was an old family joke. Their father was so notoriously frustrated by their mother's helicoptering behavior that he'd periodically claim he was going to pack up his battered army bag and run away like a disgruntled teen. One time, when Abby and Allan were kids, he'd actually gotten as far as the Mirabelle Harbor train station. With a hacking cough. And a fever of nearly 103. It took their mom and the help of two neighbors to collect him in their family's minivan and shuttle him back home and into bed again—where he belonged.

So, last Thursday, when their father tripped over an uncoiled garden hose in the backyard and fell onto the concrete patio, Allan met their parents at the clinic, noted the panicked look on both of their faces when the doc assessed the damage, and called Abby at once.

"We've got a situation up here," he said. "Any chance you can come home and help me run interference with the folks for a week or two?"

Abby spent the next two days rearranging job commitments at Floriday Vacations, the travel agency she worked at in Sarasota, and asking her best friends in town—Joy Canton, Lorelei Beck, and Marianna Gregory— to keep an eye on her condo and her soon-to-be-wilting houseplants.

She also worked part time at Joy's shop, The Beaded Periwinkle, but her friends didn't think twice about covering for her there. Marianna, who was originally from Mirabelle Harbor and who also split her time between Floriday Vacations and The Beaded Periwinkle, offered to work as many extra shifts for Abby as needed.

"Family is the most important thing," Marianna had said with a reassuring shoulder squeeze. "Go take care of your parents first. We'll muddle along here all right for a week or so."

"It just won't be nearly as fun without you," Joy said. "So don't forget to call and text us. We'll be thinking about you. And wondering what fresh mischief your brother is up to."

"Yeah," Lorelei added. "We remember all of those wild stories about Allan and his high school friends. Like a bunch of characters in a 'MacGyver' episode."

It was true. Allan had always run with quite the geeky and creative crowd. How could she ever forget the hair-raising science fun of their youth...or his best buddy,

"Rocket Rick" Zimmerman?

Abby glanced over at her brother as he navigated the left turn at an intersection, his cool confidence behind the wheel indicative of his command of all things mechanical, chemical, electrical, and combustible. At thirty-one, he was two years older than she, and in and out of more relationships than the lead singer of an alt-rock band. But despite his lack of punctuality and his tendency to cause inexplicable explosions at work, his boss at the chemical engineering lab *loved* him. If anyone could create cutting-edge technology and revolutionize the field, it was her brilliant bro, Allan.

As they passed through the lakeside suburbs surrounding Mirabelle Harbor and then, finally, into their hometown proper, her brother nudged her. "Is it weird to be back?"

"A little. Sure," she admitted. Not that she hadn't seen her parents or her brother in the six-plus years since she drove away from Mirabelle Harbor, alongside her ex-boyfriend, Chandler Michaelsen. But it had been a *long* while since she'd seen her family *here*.

An avalanche of memories cascaded through her brain as she and Allan wound their way across town. Rick...Chandler...her younger self... Oh, hell.

Was it good to be back home—or not?

Too early to say.

STORY EXCERPTS

TAKE A CHANCE ON ME (MIRABELLE HARBOR, BOOK 1) – OUT NOW!

Welcome to Mirabelle Harbor! In this scenic suburb on Chicago's North Shore, overlooking the sparkling waters of Lake Michigan, the Michaelsen family has made their home for generations. Although their parents and grandparents are now gone, siblings Derek, Blake, Sharlene, and the twins—Chandler and Chance—all have fond memories of growing up in town, and most still live there.

Chance Michaelsen, the youngest member of the family (by two minutes) and the quietest (by far), is a dedicated twenty-eight-year-old personal trainer at the local gym. While he might not say much, Chance has made it clear that he's not a fan of toxic people, unhealthy habits, or sharing too many of his emotions. With anybody.

Enter Antonia "Nia" Pappayiannis—the prettiest member of the loudest and most overly demonstrative family in town. They're also the owners of The Gala, a Greek restaurant and bakery known for its decadent pastries and located just a few steps from Chance's gym. He considers their entire family business to be the enemy of good health, but he can't quite shake his attraction to Nia, who doesn't seem nearly as impressed with him or his sculpted physique as most of the women around Mirabelle Harbor.

Unfortunately, between her doctor's orders and the

interfering ways of Chance's crazy-making ex-girlfriend, who just happens to be one of Nia's long-time friends, Chance gets assigned to be Nia's fitness coach for the month. Pure torture. And if his ex weren't already causing enough problems, he also has to deal with Nia's current boyfriend—some hotshot Chicago CEO who talks big but, in Chance's opinion, is as fake as a Styrofoam barbell.

The road to romance is going to be a rocky one, and though Nia has her doubts about getting involved, Chance has a well-developed competitive streak and might just be willing to give it a shot...if he can convince her to do the same.

In matters of the heart, would you risk it all? TAKE A CHANCE ON ME, a Mirabelle Harbor story.

<u>From the Novel:</u>

I couldn't dismiss Chance's gaze. He was watching my every movement, noticing each inch of exposed skin, which wasn't much on my side, really. The white towels gave comprehensive coverage. They were jumbo sized, so only my shoulders, arms, lower thighs, calves, and feet were visible.

But Chance took in every bit, and I squirmed under that level of scrutiny.

We sat in silence for a long time.

Finally, he cleared his throat. "So, Nia, is Grant Jordan still your boyfriend?"

I shook my head. I hadn't said any official breakup words to Grant, which would really be more like, "Hey, I don't think we should hang out for a few hours during the weekend anymore." Our relationship had hardly been the stuff of soulmates. But, after tonight, I knew I didn't want to go back to Grant's large but lonely mansion.

"My parents liked him a lot, though," I explained to Chance. "They'll be disappointed."

He narrowed his eyes. "Are *you* disappointed?"

"No."

He abruptly stood up and walked over to me. With no shirt fabric as a shield, there was nothing that could camouflage his incredibly buff upper body. Bet he did more than torso twists to get that six pack, huh? Even more than wanting to touch him, though, I wanted to know what he was thinking. My attention kept getting drawn back to his face. To his inquisitive hazel eyes.

He stood in front of me and pulled me to standing. "Turn around," he whispered.

"Why?" I murmured, glancing at the door. There was an oval sliver of a window where people walking by could peek in on us, if they were so inclined.

"I'm going to rub your shoulders," he said simply. "Don't worry. I'll stop anytime you want, but now's the best time to loosen those tight muscles. You can lean against the wall for balance."

There was almost nothing in the world I wanted more than to feel Chance's hands on my skin. Between his nearness to me, my anticipation of his touch, and the blazing temperature of the sauna, I could only take quick, shallow breaths but, nevertheless, I turned around.

From the very second his fingertips connected with the top of my shoulders, it was all I could do not to gasp or moan. He had magic hands, that man. A grip that was strong, firm, but not pinching. My neck and shoulders had never felt better.

I could only imagine what he could do to my back if I were to throw the towel on the floor and let him rub whatever he wanted, or wherever he wanted. Aunt Helen would be evoking all kinds of prayers to the blessed Virgin if she knew what I was thinking.

"You really missed your calling," I managed to say.

Chance made that low chuckling sound that sent a bolt of desire from my ears to my toenails. "I have some background in deep tissue and Swedish massage," he told me. "Board certified, actually. But I'm very selective in choosing my clientele for that service."

The air in the sauna must have hit about three thousand degrees when he spoke. I was burning up. But he continued to rub only above the towel line. Nothing remotely inappropriate. And his self-control made me want to scream, "Go lower! Push the towel down, Chance. Tell me you want me half as much as I want you."

Instead, I just sighed, and his fingers stilled. *No!*

He very gently turned me around to face him, lowered his head until his lips were millimeters from mine, and whispered, "Number 127 Arpeggio Avenue. Apartment 3."

"What?" I asked. There was steam all around us and, more than that, my brain was in a fog.

"That's my address. Just two blocks south of here." He paused. "It's your choice, Nia. But remember your question when we were texting tonight? When you asked if I was propositioning you?"

I nodded. Oh, yes. I remembered. *If I were propositioning you, I'd say to meet me at my apartment…*

"So," he said slowly, "if you would like, meet me at my apartment." Then Chance smiled, stepped away from me, and walked out of the sauna.

❀❉❀

THE ONE THAT I WANT (BOOK 2) – OUT NOW!

The summer after her beloved husband died in a car accident, Julia Meriwether Crane is still picking up the pieces of her life in Mirabelle Harbor and trying to help her ten-year-old daughter adjust to this difficult new reality.

After her best friend Sharlene—one of the well-connected Michaelsen siblings—talks her into finally going out on the town again, Julia finds herself stunned to be the object of interest of several different men: The boy who'd broken her heart back in high school. The college ex she'd left behind. And most surprising of all, the movie actor she'd always fantasized about but had never met in person...until now. Can one woman have more than one "great love" in the same lifetime? And, if so, how can she be sure which man that'll be?

Sometimes the person you think will be best for you isn't the one you really want. THE ONE THAT I WANT, a Mirabelle Harbor story.

From the Novel:

With the exception of my best friend Sharlene, the others in the wine bar had gone back to their conversations so, thankfully, I didn't have too many people witnessing my fumbles with setting up a (sort-of) date for the first time in twelve years. It was awkward, but I agreed to coffee with my old high-school boyfriend and gave Kristopher my phone number, which he dutifully punched into his cell so we could arrange a time and day to meet later.

Shar nudged me when he wasn't looking and whispered, "See? Not so hard, is it?"

I made a face at her and shrugged.

Finally, the party at The Lounge was beginning to break up. I was mentally congratulating myself on making it through the evening when the very sweet, well-dressed woman—Elsie was her name—wolf whistled. "Wait, people!"

Everyone halted.

"I've been wanting to tell you this good news all night." She paused for effect. "You know my friend Rosemary, the one who works at the Knightsbridge Theater in the city, right?"

Most of the group nodded, seeming to have met Elsie's friend or, at least, heard about her.

"There's a dress rehearsal for their upcoming summer production, 'The Bachelor Pad,' this Thursday at six thirty in the evening, in advance of next Friday's Opening Night," Elsie said. "And Rosemary reserved a block of seats for us."

Despite the noise in the wine bar, an audible spike in sound came on the heels of those words, and a couple of the women actually squealed.

I squinted at them. I mean, tickets to a play were always nice, but wasn't this taking theatrical enthusiasm a bit far?

"But that's not all," Elsie continued enthusiastically. "Rosemary also got us passes to meet the cast, just as she did for that steampunk musical last year—"

"Steampunk musical?" I hissed in Shar's ear.

She nodded. "It was bizarre. Tell you more about it later."

I grinned and brought my glass of wine to my lips, draining it of its final swallow.

"—including a special Q&A session with the director, Zachary Leeward," Elsie added, "and with the star of the show, Dane Tyler."

I choked on the last drops of merlot, coughing so hard that Bill reached across the table to hand me a fresh glass of ice water, Shar patted me on the back, and everyone else stared at me worriedly. Except for Kristopher. He shot me a knowing look.

Yeah, of course he'd remember *that*.

"Are you okay?" Elsie asked me.

I gulped down half the water. *Oh, God. Of all the actors on the planet—Dane Tyler. Here? REALLY?*

My teen world had just materialized out of thin air, like that freaky phantom ship that came from absolutely nowhere in *Pirates of the Caribbean*. My gut twisted weirdly, and I could barely breathe. "P-Please go on," I managed to whisper.

She smiled. "So, if any of you want to go to the performance, and I know you do, let me know now, and I'll email the list of names to Rosemary in the morning."

Elsie was right. With the exception of one accountant guy, who had an out-of-town business trip next week, and a very disappointed single mom, whose kid was playing in a baseball tournament Thursday night, everyone else signed up to go.

Including *me,* at Shar's insistence. And including Kristopher.

My old high-school boyfriend leaned over the table and said with a laugh, "Well, isn't that something? Maybe, if you ask him real nice, he'll recite your favorite lines from your favorite movie to you."

"Ha," I said weakly.

"Which lines? Which movie?" Shar asked.

Before I could reply, Elise jumped in and pointed to Shar and then me. "You two want to ride down with me?"

Shar answered for both of us. "Oh, yeah!"

Although I managed to stop tripping over my own tongue and was able to thank the kind woman, I didn't succeed in making more than a few last bits of small talk. All I could do was blush furiously and think to myself, in the fevered squeaking of an adolescent schoolgirl, *OMG, I'm finally going to see Dane Tyler in person! Maybe even talk to him!*

In just one evening, three distinct memories of men from my past played out like a warped summertime version of *A Christmas Carol* in my mind. Haunting memories of relationships that I'd had or had lost or had wanted— sometimes simultaneously and always more powerfully than I'd expected—were reeling through my brain on a continuous loop, braiding my emotions with the mental film footage.

Before my best friend could ask me any more questions I didn't want to answer, I hugged her goodnight and raced into the evening, forgetting until my feet hit the pavement and I collapsed into the driver's seat of my car that I wasn't, in fact, lost in time.

That I wasn't living out some high-school fantasy.

That I wasn't a vulnerable young woman, helpless in the face of fate.

I started the engine, replayed those last three thoughts again, and shook my head.

Like hell I wasn't.

✿❀✿

YOU GIVE LOVE A BAD NAME (BOOK 3) – OUT NOW!

"Nothing but love, 24/7" is the slogan of Mirabelle Harbor's only radio station, 102.5 "LOVE" FM. On the verge of turning thirty-five, local DJ Blake Michaelsen is well-known for several reasons: his very sexy on-air voice, his omnipresent family, his eligible bachelor status, and his reputation as one of the most impulsive men in Chicago's northern suburbs.

High school French teacher and lifelong romantic Vicky Bernier is not at all wild about people who exhibit reckless conduct. (Blake.) Or men who have gigantic egos. (Blake.) Or grownups who still act like teenagers. (Blake, again.) She deals with enough adolescent behavior during the school day. Unfortunately, she's the staff advisor to the Homecoming Committee, and they've chosen him as their DJ for the big fall dance.

What happens when a man whose job it is to play love songs for a living is forced to admit his deepest secret—that he doesn't believe in true love—only to discover that the one woman who might capture his heart is the same woman who distrusts him the most?

No matter what you call it, with love there's an exception to every rule. YOU GIVE LOVE A BAD NAME, a Mirabelle Harbor story.

From the Novel:

We settled our bill and stepped outside of The Lounge just as a ruckus was getting started next door at Max's Pub.

"You asshole!" this dopey, burly, drunk guy screamed, ineffectively swinging at another drunk guy.

"You witless dickhead!" slurred the second guy. But that didn't mask his identity. As soon as he spoke, I knew who it was. Everyone did.

"Vicky, isn't that Blake Michaelsen?" Janet whispered.

"Yep," I whispered back. I'd only seen him in person once before—at a big event at the radio station this summer—and it was, literally, across a crowded room. But Blake's voice on 102.5 LOVE FM was one of the sexiest I'd ever heard. I listened to him on the radio all the time. And he was my friend Sharlene's older brother, so I knew a few additional facts about him than I might have otherwise.

Like that he was impulsive.

And loud.

And kind of a manwhore.

Then again, he had a rep in town, so most women knew these things, too. It was just that Shar had actually confirmed them for me.

Blake landed a decent punch and sent the other guy stumbling. But Dopey Dude got back up.

Oh, boy.

Shar was going to be *so* pissed when she heard about this. And she would. Probably within three minutes or less. Gossip traveled at the speed of sound in Mirabelle Harbor.

There was more yelling between the men, along with a

bunch of shouts from the sports-bar crowd surrounding them. It reminded me of the stupid hall fights I'd had the misfortune to have to try to break up at the high school. Dumb boy behavior at its finest. Guys who fought each other because they couldn't rationally reason their way through a discussion. So foolish and immature. And, worse, so painful to the people who actually cared about these cretins.

Dopey Dude landed a crushing blow to Blake's abdomen. He doubled over and fell to the pavement. Then the other guy started to seriously pummel Blake while the crowd alternately jeered, taunted, and screamed their encouragement.

I winced. Blake's dark hair was matted against his forehead with sweat and, also, with some fresh blood. He had a gash across his cheekbones, dirt on his face and neck, and more blood dripping from the corner of his mouth.

And he was devastatingly handsome, even then.

Although, with the angry eyes and the snarl on his lips, he looked like the poster child for one the French revolutionary insurgents in *Les Misérables*. If he decided to build a barricade, storm the Bastille, or lead the crowd in the first verse of "Do You Hear the People Sing?" I wouldn't dare to stand in his way.

The fact that I couldn't guess whether he'd be more like a hero or a terrorist in any uprising made me immediately uncomfortable, though. I hadn't known he'd be like this. His sister could get a little fiery sometimes, but Shar had a marshmallow heart. Blake, by contrast, looked both self-destructive and vicious. Like he could quite effectively kill someone.

Finally, an officer came on the scene and broke up the fight. He ordered us all to leave, but I was rooted to the spot. I couldn't take my eyes off Blake's cut-up face. So many bruises, and he was even spitting blood.

Lisa nudged me. "Let's go, Vicky."

Before I could make my feet move, Blake looked up at me and our gazes collided. I kept imagining the shock Shar would feel if she saw her brother in this horribly battered, sweaty, and drunken state. She was very protective of her family. But nothing was going to protect Blake from the wrath of one massive hangover and the need for some serious first aid.

His eyes turned even darker and they narrowed dangerously as he continued to stare at me.

Christine tugged me away.

"They were like a couple of wasted jocks after a football game," she observed on the drive home.

"I know. I was thinking the same thing. Like those boys that get into fights in the school cafeteria. With them, it's all crazy levels of testosterone and impaired judgment, leading to damage of property and reckless endangerment of themselves and others. Imagine someone acting that way after being out of high school for fifteen years? It's like they never got all the way through adolescence."

Christine nodded. "Although I can't say being a mature grownup all the time is a barrel of laughs."

I smiled. "True. But anything is better than being forever seventeen."

I remembered myself at seventeen and suppressed a shudder. That was one time of my life I'd *never* want to relive, and I had daily witness as to why in my classroom.

Though, if forced to be completely honest with myself, one of the main reasons I'd been drawn to teaching was to see if I could make high school a better experience for kids like me. For those quirky, quiet, culture-loving, rule-following bookworms who really wanted to learn. Not that I was so different now, really. It was just that, back then, I'd felt so alone. I hadn't realized there might be others like me out there.

At least I had good female friends. But it was too bad my male counterpart didn't seem to exist. At least not in large enough quantities to keep searching for him. There were probably only fifty straight, single, American men who'd fit my criteria for dating. And chances were high that they were spread randomly across the United States. I'd be lucky to find even one or two anywhere in Illinois. My ideal, most compatible love match was probably living in a remote town in northern New Mexico or something.

I said goodnight to Christine, went inside my apartment, and leaned against the door with a deep sigh. I should go to sleep, but I just couldn't. All I'd be able to see behind my closed eyes would be Blake Michaelsen's bloodied, infuriated face.

✿❀✿

STRANGER ON THE SHORE (BOOK 4) – OUT NOW!

On the verge of turning forty and having just lost her job, Marianna Gregory flees Mirabelle Harbor for the summer with little more than a suitcase, her beat-up car, and the blessings of her good friend Olivia Michaelsen. Her ex-husband is living a new life in California. Her college-aged daughter is spending her vacation with her boyfriend in Michigan. And the house Marianna once called her own finally sold, so she has nowhere to live in Illinois now anyway.

However, her wealthy sister Ellen owns an empty bungalow on the beach in Sarasota, Florida, so Marianna turns to the sea for a chance to go shelling, regroup, and figure out what to do with this new chapter in her life. She doesn't bargain on having to face down several family crises while she's away, nor does she count on meeting a handsome beachcomber who bears a striking resemblance to Elvis. Just as surprising is the craft project she gets roped into volunteering for and the new group of friends who might just change the way she views the world and her future.

The most unexpected gifts can be found where the land meets the sea. STRANGER ON THE SHORE, a Mirabelle Harbor story.

From the Novel:

A mix of cerulean with teal for the furthest watery depths.

A dabbling of silvery sunlight, whiting out patches of sea and sand like a spotlight.

Gil Canton studied the shoreline with the practiced eye of an artist. Which was what he was, he reminded himself. Never mind the low, deep voice from decades' past that told him otherwise. That told him he should be using his powers of observation on "a worthier, more lucrative cause."

Bullshit.

A faint blend of burnt umber and goldenrod in a subtle line underscoring the crisp cottony tufts of rolling waves.

A flash of gray and green as the sunfish tangled with the seaweed just below the surface.

Anyone with a heart knew the creatures of the ocean were as *worthy* as anything out in the world. That the Gulf was not only a visual feast for a painter, but it was a composer's symphony, a poet's playground.

Anyone with a heart...ahh. But that was the problem, wasn't it?

Gil grimaced. Calf-deep in the warm water and strolling languidly along the Siesta Key shoreline, he picked up his stride to outrace that old, familiar voice. It didn't work. It never the hell worked. But he turned his attention to the passersby in hopes of a distraction.

Shades of skin color in a palette of creams, tans,

bronzes, chocolates and, sometimes, sunburned reds.

The fascinating discordance of fabric hues and textures and patterns, draping the wearer in a manner that left no question as to whether the individual wanted to be noticed...or wanted to blend into the seascape.

He knew he looked at the beach differently than he had when he'd first moved here twenty-six years ago. And, unlike the appreciative but unobservant gazes of the bikini-clad tourists, he needed to distinguish between the various ranges of blues and greens, the buffet of multicolored accessory images and the differing degrees of whiteness from the sand to the bungalows—for the sake of his passion. His paintings.

Why was it so easy, so natural for him to be both loving and discerning in one area of his life but not in another?

With a canvas, he could step back and assess it. If he saw he'd done something wrong or, more frequently, had neglected to do something completely right, he would be able to see the problem area with the help of a few feet of distance and, then, correct it.

With relationships—parental, romantic, professional or otherwise—it was never that simple. Stepping back was harder for the other person to accept. And it tended to create more damage, even when the objective was to do just the opposite. To achieve a fresh perspective. Clarity.

Art and life? Not so much the same.

He kicked lightly at a broken conch with the tip of his water shoe. Even with a chunk of its shell missing, it was still beautiful. There was almost heartbreaking beauty on this shore.

Seagulls squawking above and around him in a flying dance of circles and landings.

Children splashing and frolicking, often with a battalion of siblings and water toys.

An old woman dressed all in white, someone he'd seen many times, stood several yards from him, chatting with an attractive younger lady—an obvious newcomer. He couldn't help but check out the new woman. She was a tad overdressed in her pinkish t-shirt and navy shorts. Untanned and pensive. Awed by the Gulf setting in that mystified tourist sort of way. The coast was full of visitors like that. Nothing wrong with them, he supposed. His business depended on them, after all. But it was hard to get to know many people well in such a transient environment.

With a shrug, he returned his focus to the water—the rhythmic breaking of the waves trying their darnedest to drown out his father's voice once and for all until, a few minutes later, a sound he couldn't ignore pierced his concentration.

Up Next:
LOOK FOR THE RETURN OF BOTH ABBY SOLINSKI AND CHANDLER MICHAELSEN TO THEIR HOMETOWN IN UPCOMING MIRABELLE HARBOR STORIES, AS WELL AS CHANCE & NIA'S ROMANTIC CHRISTMAS WEDDING WITH ALL OF THEIR FAMILY AND FRIENDS!!

Learn more about the Mirabelle Harbor books on Marilyn's website page for the series:

www.marilynbrant.com/books/the-mirabelle-harbor-series/

The Mirabelle Harbor Series

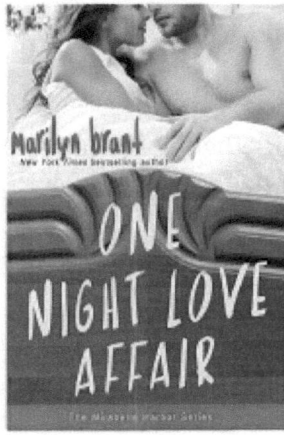

Bonus Crossover Novella

ABOUT THE AUTHOR

Marilyn Brant has been told she writes with honesty, liveliness and wit (descriptors she's grown terribly fond of) about complex, intelligent women—like her friends—and their significant personal relationships. Although her favorite pursuits undoubtedly involve books, she proves she's not just a literary snob by confessing her lifelong fascination (read: obsession) with popular music, especially from the '70s and '80s, most flavors of ice cream, and a variety of sensuous body lotions/oils.

As a former teacher, library staff member, freelance magazine writer, and national book reviewer, Marilyn has spent much of her life lost in literature. She is the *New York Times* and *USA Today* bestselling and award-winning author of twelve novels and three novellas to date, and a lifetime member of the Jane Austen Society of North America. The Illinois Association of Teachers of English (IATE) selected her as their 2013 Author of the Year.

Her debut coming-of-age novel, *ACCORDING TO JANE* (Kensington, 2009), featuring the ghost of Jane Austen giving a young woman dating advice, won the Romance Writers of America's prestigious Golden Heart Award and the Booksellers' Best, and it was named one of the "Top 100 Romance Novels of All Time" by Buzzle.com. Her second novel, *FRIDAY MORNINGS AT NINE* (Kensington, 2010), was a Doubleday and Book-of-the-Month Club pick in women's fiction. *A SUMMER IN EUROPE* (Kensington, 2011) was featured in the Literary Guild and BOMC2, and it became a Top 20 Bestseller in Fiction and Literature for the Rhapsody Book Club. The Polish translation of the novel was released in June 2013.

She's also a #1 Kindle & #1 Nook bestseller, who writes fun and flirty romantic comedies, like her stories in

THE SWEET TEMPTATIONS COLLECTION, that involve sweet treats, unexpected love, and large doses of humor. *THE ROAD TO YOU*—a coming-of-age romantic mystery—was selected as one of the Top 20 Best Books of the Year (December 2013) by The Reading Frenzy. Now she's at work on the "Mirabelle Harbor" romance series: Look for books *TAKE A CHANCE ON ME, THE ONE THAT I WANT, YOU GIVE LOVE A BAD NAME, STRANGER ON THE SHORE, ONE NIGHT LOVE AFFAIR*, and more! And be sure to check out her short story, "When Life Imitates Art," in RWA's upcoming anthology, *SECOND CHANCES* (tentative title), edited by international bestselling author Sylvia Day.

Marilyn currently lives in the Chicago suburbs with her family. When she isn't reading her friends' books or watching old movies, she's working on her next novel, eating chocolate indiscriminately, and hiding from the laundry.

Please visit her website: www.MarilynBrant.com.